Praise For
RUTH RENDELL
AND
THE
COPPER
PEACOCK

A N D   O T H E R   S T O R I E S

more . . .

"Ms. Rendell's signature is the malevolence of the day-to-day, shot through with currents of wit and whimsy."
—*Richmond Times-Dispatch*

"If the crime short story is an endangered species, Ruth Rendell is one of the few courageous environmentalists fighting for its survival. She presents irrefutable evidence that the genre deserves not merely to survive, but to flourish."
—*The Times,* London

"Rendell terrorizes with the subtle authority of a cat burglar in the night."
—*San Francisco Chronicle*

"Rendell writes compelling studies in character, ringing new changes on the concept of the whydunit, feeding the reader wickedly self-revealing clues about the reasons people act as they do."
—*New York Times Book Review*

"The finest living author of psychological suspense."
—*Chicago Sun-Times*

"Absolutely stunning."
—*Washington Post Book World*

"Rendell's pacing is superb, her characters extraordinarily vivid."
—*Cosmopolitan*

"Undoubtedly one of the best writers of English mystery."
—*Los Angeles Times*

"Rendell has been demonically successful exploring obsessiveness, especially madness fueled by love...a master of the shuddery detail."
—*Newsweek*

"It's clear why so many fellow mystery writers regard Rendell as a model."
—*Wall Street Journal*

RUTH RENDELL

THE COPPER PEACOCK

AND OTHER STORIES

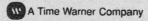

THE MYSTERIOUS PRESS

New York • Tokyo • Sweden

Published by Warner Books

A Time Warner Company

MYSTERIOUS PRESS EDITION

Copyright © 1991 by Kingsmarkham Enterprises Ltd.
All rights reserved.
This work was first published in Great Britain by Century Hutchinson, Ltd., London.

Cover design by Jackie Merri Meyer
Cover illustration by Mel Odom

The Mysterious Press name and logo are trademarks of Warner Books, Inc.

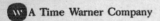 Mysterious Press Books are published by Warner Books, Inc.
1271 Avenue of the Americas
New York, NY 10020

W A Time Warner Company

Printed in the United States of America

Originally published in hardcover by The Mysterious Press.
First Printed in Paperback: September, 1992
10 9 8 7 6 5 4 3 2

A Pair of
Yellow
Lilies

A famous designer, young still, who first became well-known when she made a princess's wedding dress, was coming to speak to the women's group of which Bridget Thomas was secretary. She would be the second speaker in the autumn programme, which was devoted to success and how women had achieved it. Repeated requests on Bridget's part for a biography from Annie Carter so that she could provide her members with interesting background information had met with no response. Bridget had even begun to wonder if she would remember to come and give her talk in three weeks' time. Meanwhile, obliged to do her own research, she had gone into the public library to look Annie Carter up in *Who's Who*.

Bridget had a precarious job in a small and not very prosperous bookshop. In her mid-thirties, with a rather pretty face that often looked worried and worn, she thought that she might learn something from this current series of talks. Secrets of success might be imparted, blueprints for achievement, even short cuts to prosperity. She never had enough money, never knew security, could not have dreamt of aspiring to an Annie Carter ready-to-wear even when such a garment had been twice marked down in a sale. Clothes, anyway, were hardly a priority, coming a long way down the list of essentials that was headed by rent, fares, food, in that order.

In the library she was not noticeable. She was not, in any case and anywhere, the kind of woman on whom second glances were bestowed. On this Wednesday evening, when the shop closed at its normal time and the library later than usual, she could be seen, by those few who cared to look, wearing a long black skirt with a dusty appearance, a T-shirt of a slightly different shade of black—it had been washed fifty times at least—and a waistcoat in dark striped cotton. Her shoes were black velvet Chinese slippers with instep straps, and there was a hole she did not know about in her turquoise-blue tights, low down on the left calf. Bridget's hair was wispy, long and fair, worn in loops. She was carrying an enormous black leather bag, capacious and heavy, and full of unnecessary things. Herself the first to admit this, she often said she meant to make changes in the matter of this bag but she never got around to it.

This evening the bag contained a number of crumpled tissues, some pink, some white; a spray bottle of Wild Musk cologne; three ballpoint pens; a pair of nail-scissors; a pair of nail-clippers; a London tube pass; a British Telecom phone card; an address book; a mascara wand in a shade called After-Midnight Blue; a cheque-book; a notebook; a postcard from a friend on holiday in Brittany; a calculator; a paperback of Vasari's *Lives of the Artists*, which Bridget had always meant to read but was not getting on very fast with; a container of nasal spray; a bunch of keys; a book of matches; a silver ring with a green stone, probably onyx; a pheasant's feather picked up while staying for the weekend in someone's cottage in Somerset; three quarters of a bar of milk chocolate; a pair of sun-glasses; and her wallet—which contained the single credit card she possessed, her bank cheque card, her library card, her never-needed driving-licence, and seventy pounds, give or take a little, in five- and ten-pound notes. There was also about four pounds in change.

On the previous evening Bridget had been to see her aunt. This was the reason for her carrying so much money. Bridget's Aunt Monica was an old woman who had never married and whom her brother, Bridget's father, referred to with brazen insensitivity as "a maiden lady." Bridget thought this outrageous and remonstrated with her father but was unable to bring him to see anything offensive in this expression. Though Monica had never had a husband, she had been successful in other areas of life, and might indeed almost have qualified to join Bridget's list of female achievers fit to speak to her women's group. Inherited money wisely invested brought her in a substantial income, and this, added to the pension derived from having been quite high up the ladder in the Civil Service, made her nearly rich.

Bridget did not like taking Monica Thomas's money. Or she told herself she didn't, actually meaning that she liked the money very much but felt humiliated, as a young, healthy woman who ought to have been able to keep herself adequately, taking money from an old one who had done so and still did. Monica, not invariably during these visits but often enough, would ask her how she was managing.

"Making ends meet, are you?" was the form this inquiry usually took.

Bridget felt a little tide of excitement rising in her at these words because she knew they signified a coming munificence. She simultaneously felt ashamed at being excited by such a thing. This was the way, she believed, other women might feel at the prospect of love-making or discovering themselves pregnant or getting promoted. She felt excited because her old aunt, her maiden aunt tucked away in a gloomy flat in Fulham, was about to give her fifty pounds.

Characteristically, Monica prepared the ground. "You may as well have it now instead of waiting till I'm gone."

And Bridget would smile and look away, or, if she felt brave, tell her aunt not to talk about dying. Once she had gone so far as to say, "I don't come here for the sake of what you give me, you know," but as she put this into words she knew she did. And Monica, replying tartly, "And I don't see my little gifts as paying you for your visits," must have known that she did and they did, and that the two of them were involved in a commercial transaction, calculated enough, but imbued with guilt and shame.

Bridget always felt that at her age, thirty-six, and her aunt's, seventy-two, it should be she who gave alms and her aunt who received them. That was the usual way of things. Here the order was reversed, and with a hand that she had to restrain forcibly from trembling with greed and need and excitement, she had reached out on the previous evening for the notes that were presented as a sequel to another of Monica's favourite remarks: that she would like to see Bridget better-dressed. With only a vague grasp of changes in the cost of living, Monica nevertheless knew that for any major changes in her niece's wardrobe to take place, a larger-than-usual sum would be required. Another twenty-five had been added to the customary fifty. Five pounds or so had been spent during the course of the day. Bridget had plenty to do with the rest, which did not include buying the simple dark coat and skirt and pink twin set Monica had suggested. There was the gas bill, for instance, and the chance at last of settling the credit-card account, on which interest was being paid at 21 per cent. Not that Bridget had no wistful thoughts of beautiful things she would like to possess and most likely never would. A chair in a shop window in Bond Street, for instance, a chair that stood alone in slender, almost arrogant, elegance, with its high-stepping legs and sweetly curved back, she imagined gracing her room as a bringer of daily renewed happiness and pride. Only today a woman had come into the shop to order the new Salman Rushdie and she had been wearing a dress that was unmistakably Annie Carter. Bridget had gazed at that dress as at some unattainable glory, at its bizarreries of zips round the sleeves and triangles excised from armpits, uneven hem-line and slashed back, for if the truth were told it was the fantastic she admired in such matters and would not have been seen dead in a pink twin set.

She had gazed and longed, just as now, fetching *Who's Who* back to her seat at the table, she had stared, in passing, at the back of a glorious jacket. Afterwards she could not have said if it was a man or woman wearing it, a person in jeans was all she could have guessed at. The person in jeans was pressed fairly close up against the science fiction shelves so that the back of the jacket, its most beautiful and striking area, was displayed to the best advantage. The jacket was made of blue denim with a design appliquéd on it. Bridget knew the work was appliqué because she had learned something of this technique herself at a handicrafts class, all part of the horizon-widening, life-enhancing programme with which she combated loneliness. Patches of satin and silk and brocade had been used in the work, and beads and sequins and gold thread as well. The design was of a flock of brilliant butterflies, purple and turquoise and vermilion and royal blue and fuchsia pink, tumbling and fluttering from the open mouths of a pair of yellow lilies. Bridget had gazed at this fantastic picture in silks and jewels and then looked quickly away, resolving to look no more, she desired so much to possess it herself.

Annie Carter's *Who's Who* entry mentioned a book she had written on fashion in the early eighties. Bridget thought it would be sensible to acquaint herself with it. It would provide her with something to talk about when she and the committee entertained the designer to supper after her talk. Leaving *Who's Who* open on the table and her bag wedged between the table legs and the leg of her chair, Bridget went off to consult the library's computer as to whether this book was in stock.

Afterwards she recalled, though dimly, some of the people she had seen as she crossed the floor of the library to where the computer was. An old man in gravy-brown clothes reading a newspaper, two old women in fawn raincoats and pudding-basin hats, a child that ran about in defiance of its mother's threats and pleas. The mother was a woman about Bridget's own age, grossly fat, with fuzzy dark hair and swollen legs. There had been other people less memorable. The computer told her the book was in stock but out on loan. Bridget went back to her table and sat down. She read the sparse *Who's Who* entry once more, noting that Annie Carter's interests were bob-sleighing and collecting *netsuke*, which seemed to make her rather a daunting person, and then she reached down for her bag and the notebook it contained.

The bag was gone.

The feeling Bridget experienced is one everyone has when they lose something important or think they have lost it, the shock of loss. It was a physical sensation as of something falling through her—turning over in her chest first and then tumbling down inside her body and out through the soles of her feet. She immediately told herself she couldn't have lost the bag, she couldn't have, it couldn't have been stolen—who would have stolen it among that company? She must have taken it with her to the computer. Bridget went back to the computer, she ran back, and the bag wasn't there. She told the two assistant librarians and then the librarian herself and they all looked round the library for the bag. It seemed to Bridget that by this time everyone else who had been in the library had swiftly disappeared, everyone, that is, but the old man reading the newspaper.

The librarian was extremely kind. They were about to close and she said she would go to the police with Bridget, it was on her way. Bridget continued to feel the shock of loss, sickening overturnings in her body and sensations of panic and disbelief. Her head seemed too lightly poised on her neck, almost as if it floated.

"It can't have happened," she kept saying to the librarian. "I just don't believe it could have happened in those few seconds I was away."

"I'm afraid it did," said the librarian, who was too kind to say anything about Bridget's unwisdom in leaving the bag unattended even for a few seconds. "It's nothing to do with me, but was there much money in it?"

"Quite a lot. Yes, quite a lot." Bridget added humbly, "Well, a lot for me."

The police could offer very little hope of recovering the money. The bag, they said, and some of its contents might turn up. Meanwhile Bridget had no means of getting into her room, no means even of phoning the credit-card company to notify them of the theft. The librarian, whose name was Elizabeth Derwent, saw to all that. She took Bridget to her own home and led her to the telephone and then took her to a locksmith. It was the beginning of what was to be an enduring friendship. Bridget might have lost many of her worldly goods, but as she said afterwards to her Aunt Monica, at least she got Elizabeth's friendship out of it.

"It's an ill wind that blows nobody any good," said Monica, pressing fifty pounds in ten-pound notes into Bridget's hand.

But all this was in the future. That first evening Bridget had to come to terms with the loss of seventy pounds, her driving-licence, her credit card, her cheque-book, the *Lives of the Artists* (she would never read it now), her address book, and the silver ring with the stone that was probably onyx. She mourned, alone there in her room. She fretted miserably, shock and disbelief having been succeeded by the inescapable certainty that someone had deliberately stolen her bag. Several cups of strong hot tea comforted her a little. Bridget had more in common with her aunt than she would have liked to think possible, being very much a latter-day maiden lady in every respect but maiden-hood.

At the end of the week a parcel came. It contained her wallet (empty but for the library card), the silver ring, her address book, her notebook, the nail-scissors and the nail-clippers, the mascara wand in the shade called After-Midnight Blue, and most of the things she had lost but for the money and the credit card and the cheque-book, the driving-licence, the paperback Vasari, and the bag itself. A letter accompanied the things. It said:

Dear Miss Thomas,

This name and address were in the notebook. I hope they are yours and that this will reach you. I found your things inside a plastic bag on top of a litter-bin in Kensington Church Street. It was the wallet which made me think they were not things someone had meant to throw away. I am afraid this is absolutely all there was, though I have the feeling there was money in the wallet and perhaps other valuable things. Yours sincerely,

Patrick Baker.

His address and a phone number headed the sheet of paper. Bridget, who was not usually impulsive, was so immediately brimming with amazed happiness and restored faith in human nature that she lifted the phone at once and dialled the number. He answered. It was a pleasant voice, educated, rather slow and deliberate in its enunciation of words, a young man's voice. She poured out her gratitude. How kind he was! What trouble he had been to! Not only to retrieve her things but to take them home, to parcel them up, pay the postage, stand in a queue no doubt at the Post Office! What could she do for him? How could she show the gratitude she felt?

Come and have a drink with me, he said. Well, of course she would, of course. She promised to have a drink with him and a place was arranged and a time, though she was already getting cold feet. She consulted Elizabeth.

"Having a drink in a pub in Kensington High Street couldn't do any harm," said Elizabeth, smiling.

"It's not really something I do." It wasn't something she had done for years, at any rate. In fact, it was two years since Bridget had even been out with a man, since her sad affair with the married accountant, which had dragged on year after year, had finally come to an end. Drinking in pubs had not been a feature of the relationship. Sometimes they had made swift furtive love in the small office where clients' VAT files were kept. "I suppose," she said, "it might make a pleasant change."

The aspect of Patrick Baker that would have made him particularly attractive to most women, if it did not repel Bridget, at least put her off. He was too good-looking for her. He was, in fact, radiantly beautiful, like an angel or a young Swedish tennis player. This, of course, did not specially matter that first time. But his looks registered with her as she walked across the little garden at the back of the pub and he rose from the table at which he was sitting. His looks frightened her and made her shy. It would not have been true, though, to say that she could not keep her eyes off him. Looking at him was altogether too much for her, it was almost an embarrassment, and she tried to keep her eyes turned away.

Nor would she have known what to say to him. Fortunately, he was eager to recount in detail his discovery of her property in the litter-bin in Kensington Church Street. Bridget was good at listening and she listened. He told her also how he had once lost a brief-case in a tube train and a friend of his had had his wallet stolen on a train going from New York to Philadelphia. Emboldened by these homely and not at all sophisticated anecdotes, Bridget told him about the time her Aunt Monica had had burglars and lost an emerald necklace, which fortunately had been insured. This prompted him to ask more about her aunt and Bridget found herself being quite amusing, recounting Monica's financial adventures. She didn't see why she shouldn't tell him the origins of the stolen money and he seemed interested when she said it came from Monica, who was in the habit of bestowing like sums on her.

"You see, she says I'm to have it one day—she means when she's dead, poor dear—so why not now?"

"Why not indeed?"

"It was just my luck to have my wallet stolen the day after she'd given me all that money."

He asked her to have dinner with him. Bridget said all right but it mustn't be anywhere expensive or grand. She asked Elizabeth what she should wear. They were in a clothes mood, for it was the evening of the Annie Carter talk to the women's group, which Elizabeth had been persuaded to join.

"He doesn't dress at all formally himself," Bridget said. "Rather the reverse." He and she had been out for another drink in the meantime. "He was wearing this kind of safari suit with a purple shirt. But oh, Elizabeth, he is amazing to look at. Rather too much so, if you know what I mean."

Elizabeth didn't. She said that surely one couldn't be too good-looking? Bridget said she knew she was being silly but it embarrassed her a bit—well, being seen with him, if Elizabeth knew what she meant. It made her feel awkward.

"I'll lend you my black lace if you like," Elizabeth said. "It would suit you and it's suitable for absolutely everything."

Bridget wouldn't borrow the black lace. She refused to sail in under anyone else's colours. She wouldn't borrow Aunt Monica's emerald necklace either, the one she had bought to replace the necklace the burglars took. Her black skirt and the velvet top from the second-hand shop in Hammersmith would be quite good enough. If she couldn't have an Annie Carter she would rather not compromise. Monica, who naturally had never been told anything about the married accountant or his distant predecessor, the married primary school teacher, spoke as if Patrick Baker were the first man Bridget had ever been alone with, and spoke too as if marriage were a far-from-remote possibility. Bridget listened to all this while thinking how awful it would be if she were to fall in love with Patrick Baker and become addicted to his beauty and suffer when separated from him.

Even as she thought in this way, so prudently and with irony, she could see his face before her, its hawk-like lineaments and its softnesses, the wonderful mouth and the large wide-set eyes, the hair that was fair and thick and the skin that was smooth and brown. She saw too his muscular figure, slender and graceful yet strong, his long hands and his tapering fingers, and she felt something long suppressed, a prickle of desire that plucked very lightly at the inside of her and made her gasp a little.

The restaurant where they had their dinner was not grand or expensive, and this was just as well since at the end of the meal Patrick found that he had left his cheque-book at home and Bridget was obliged to pay for their dinner out of the money Monica had given her to buy an evening dress. He was very grateful. He kissed her on the pavement outside the restaurant, or, if not quite outside it, under the arch-way that was the entrance to the mews. They went back to his place in a taxi.

Patrick had quite a nice flat at the top of a house in Bayswater, not exactly overlooking the park but nearly. It was interesting what was happening to Bridget. Most of the time she was able to stand outside herself and view these deliberate acts of hers with detachment. She would have the pleasure of him, he was so beautiful, she would have it and that would be that. Such men were not for her, not at any rate for more than once or twice. But if she could once in a lifetime have one of them for once or twice, why not? Why not?

The life too, the life-style, was not for her. On the

whole she was better off at home with a pot of strong hot tea and her embroidery or the latest paperback on changing attitudes to women in western society. Nor had she any intention of sharing Aunt Monica's money when the time came. She had recently had to be stern with herself about a tendency, venal and degrading, to dream of that distant prospect when she would live in a World's End studio with a gallery, fit setting for the arrogant Bond Street chair, and dress in a bold eccentric manner, in flowing skirts and antique pelisses and fine old lace.

Going home with Patrick, she was rather drunk. Not drunk enough not to know what she was doing but drunk enough not to care. She was drunk enough to shed her inhibitions while being sufficiently sober to know she had inhibitions, to know that they would be waiting to return to her later and to return quite unchanged. She went into Patrick's arms with delight, with the reckless abandon and determination to enjoy herself, of someone embarking on a world cruise that must necessarily take place but once. Being in bed with him was not in the least like being in the VAT records office with the married accountant. She had known it would not be and that was why she was there. During the night the central heating went off and failed, through some inadequacy of a fragile pilot light, to restart itself. It grew cold but Bridget, in the arms of Patrick Baker, did not feel it.

She was the first to wake up. Bridget was the kind of person who is always the first to wake up. She lay in bed a little way apart from Patrick Baker and thought about what a lovely time she had had the night before and how that was enough and she would not see him again. Seeing him again might be dangerous and she could not afford, with her unmemorable appearance, her precarious job and low wage, to put herself in peril. Presently she got up and said to Patrick, who had stirred a little and made an attempt in a kindly way to cuddle her, that she would make him a cup of tea.

Patrick put his nose out of the bedclothes and said it was freezing, the central heating had gone wrong, it was always going wrong. "Don't get cold," he said sleepily. "Find something to put on in the cupboard."

Even if they had been in the tropics Bridget would not have dreamt of walking about a man's flat with no clothes on. She dressed. While the kettle was boiling she looked with interest around Patrick's living-room. There had been no opportunity to take any of it in on the previous evening. He was an untidy man, she noted, and his taste was not distinguished. You could see he bought his pictures ready-framed at Athena Art. He hadn't many books and most of what he had was science fiction, so it was rather a surprise to come upon Vasari's *Lives of the Artists* in paperback between a volume of fighting fantasy and a John Wyndham classic.

Perhaps she did, after all, feel cold. She was aware of a sudden unpleasant chill. It was comforting to feel the warmth of the kettle against her hands. She made the tea and took him a cup, setting it down on the bedside table, for he was fast asleep again. Shivering now, she opened the cupboard door and looked inside.

He seemed to possess a great many coats and jackets. She pushed the hangers along the rail, sliding tweed to brush against serge and linen against wild silk. His wardrobe was vast and complicated. He must have a great deal to spend on himself. The jacket with the butterflies slid into sudden brilliant view, as if

pushed there by some stage-manager of fate. Everything conspired to make the sight of it dramatic, even
the sun, which came out and shed an unexpected ray
into the open cupboard. Bridget gazed at the denim
jacket as she had gazed with similar lust and wonder
once before. She stared at the cascade of butterflies in
vermilion and purple turquoise, royal blue and fuchsia
pink that tumbled and fluttered from the open mouths
of a pair of yellow lilies.

She hardly hesitated before taking it off its hanger
and putting it on. It was glorious. She remembered
that this was the word she had thought of the first time
she had seen it. How she had longed to possess it and
how she had not dared look for long lest the yearning
became painful and ridiculous! With her head a little
on one side she stood over Patrick, wondering whether
to kiss him goodbye. Perhaps not, perhaps it would be
better not. After all, he would hardly notice.

She let herself out of the flat. They would not
meet again. A more than fair exchange had been
silently negotiated by her. Feeling happy, feeling very
light of heart, she ran down the stairs and out into the
morning, insulated from the cold by her coat of many
colours, her butterflies, her rightful possession.

PAPERWORK ✓

PAPERWORK

My earliest memories are of paper. I can see my grandmother sitting at the table she used for a desk, a dining-table made to seat twelve, with her scrap-book before her and the scissors in her hand. She called it her research. For years three newspapers came into that house every day and each week half a dozen magazines and periodicals. She was a diligent correspondent. Her post was large and she wrote at least one letter each day. She was a writer without hope or desire for publication. My grandfather was a solicitor in our nearest town, four miles away, and he brought work home, paperwork. He always carried two brief-cases and they bulged with documents.

Because he was a man, he had a study of his own and a proper desk. The house was quite large enough for my grandmother to have had a study too, but she would not have used that word in respect of herself. She had her table put into what they called the sewing-room, though no sewing was ever done in it in my time. She spent most of each day in there, covering reams of paper with her small handwriting or cutting things out of papers and pasting them into a succession of scrap-books. Sometimes she cut things out of books, and one of the small miseries of living in that house was to open a book in the library and find part of a chapter missing or the one poem you wanted gone from an anthology.

The sewing-room door was always left open. This was so that my grandmother might hear what was going on in the rest of the house, not to indicate that visitors would be welcome. She would hear me coming up the stairs, no matter what care I took to tread silently, and call out before I reached the open door, "No children in here, please," as if it were a school or a big family of sisters and brothers living there instead of just me.

It was a very large house, though not large enough or handsome enough to be a stately home. If visitors go there now in busloads, as I have heard they do, it is not for architecture or antiquity, but for another, uglier, reason. Eighteen fifty-one was the year of its building. The architect, if architect there was, was one of those Victorians who debased the classical and was too cowardly for the innovations of the Gothic. White bricks were the principal building material and these are not really white but the pale glabrous grey of cement. The windows were just too wide for their height, the front door too low for the fat pillars that flanked it and the hemispherical portico they supported, a plaster dome shaped like the crown of my grandfather's bowler hat and which put me in mind, when I was older, of a tomb in one of London's bigger cemeteries. Or rather, when I saw such a tomb, I would be reminded of my grandparents' house.

It was a long way from the village, at least two miles. The town, as I have said, was four miles away, and anything bigger, anywhere in which life and excitement might be going on, three times that distance. There were no buses. If you wanted to go out you went by car, and if there was no car you walked. My grandfather, wearing his bowler, drove himself and his brief-cases to work in a black Daimler. Sometimes I used to wonder how my mother had gone, when I was a baby and she left me with her parents, by what means she had made her escape. It was not my grandmother but the daily woman, Mrs. Poulter, who told me my mother had had no car of her own.

"She couldn't drive, pet. She was too young to learn, you see. You're too young to drive when you're sixteen but you're not too young to have a baby. Funny, isn't it?"

Perhaps someone had called for her. Anyway, two miles is not far to walk, and a denizen of that house would be used to walking. Had she gone in daylight or after dark? Had she discussed her departure with her parents, asked their permission to go, perhaps, or had she done what Mrs. Poulter called a moonlight flit? Sometimes I imagined her writing a note and fastening it to her pillow with the point of a knife. Notes were always being written, you see, particularly by my grandmother (to my grandfather, to Evie, Mrs. Poulter, to the tradesmen, to me when I could read handwriting, thank-you notes, and even occasionally notes of invitation), so I had experience of them from an early age, though not of knives at that time.

I used to wonder about these things, for I had plenty of time and solitude for wondering. One day I overheard my grandmother say to an acquaintance from the village (not a friend, she had no friends):

"I have never allowed myself to get fond of the child, purely as a matter of self-preservation. Suppose its mother decides to come back for it? She is its mother. She would have a right to it. And then where should I be? If I allowed myself to get fond of it, I mean?"

That was when I was about seven. A person of seven is too old to be referred to as "it." Perhaps a person of seven months or even seven days would be too old. But overhearing this did not upset me. It cheered me up and gave me hope. My mother would come for me. At least there was a strong possibility she would come, enough to keep my grandmother from loving me. And I understood somehow that she was tempted to love me. The temptation was there and she had to prevent herself from yielding to it, so that she was in a very different position from my grandfather, who, I am sure, had no temptation to resist.

It was at about this time that I took it into my head that the scrap-book my grandmother was currently working on was concerned with my mother. The newspaper cuttings and the magazine photographs were of her. She might be an actress or a model. Did my grandparents get letters from her? It was my job or Evie's to take up the post, and on my way to the dining-room, where my grandparents always had a formal breakfast together, I would examine envelopes. Most were typewritten. All the letters that came for my grandfather were typed letters in envelopes with a typed address. But regularly there came to my grandmother, every two or three weeks, a letter in a blue envelope with a London postmark and the address in a handwriting not much more formed than my own, the capitals disproportionately large and the *g*'s and *y*'s with long tails that curled round like the basenji's. I was sure these letters were from my mother and that some of them, much cut about, found their way into the scrap-book.

If children are not loved, they say, when they are little, they never learn to love. I am grateful therefore that there was one person in that house to love me and a creature whom I could love. My grandparents, you understand, were not old. My mother was sixteen when I was born, so they were still in their early forties. Of course they seemed old to me, though not old as Evie was. Even then I could appreciate that Evie belonged in quite a different generation, the age group of my schoolfellows' grandmothers.

She was some sort of relation. She may even have been my grandmother's aunt. I believe she had lived with them since they were first married as a kind of housekeeper, running things and organizing things and doing the cooking. It was her home but she was there on sufferance and she was frightened of my grandmother. When I wanted information I went to Mrs. Poulter, who was not afraid of what she said because she did not care if she got the sack.

"They need me more than I need them, pet. There's a dozen houses round here where they'd fall over themselves to get me."

The trouble was that she knew very little. She had come to work there after my mother left and what she

25

knew—as, for instance, my mother's inability to drive—was from hearsay and gossip. Her name she knew, and her age, of course, and that she had not wanted to marry my father, though my grandparents had very much wanted her to marry without being particular about whom.

"They called her Sandy. I expect it was because she had ginger hair."

"Was it the same colour as the basenji?" I said, but Mrs. Poulter could not tell me that. She had never seen my mother.

Evie was afraid to answer my questions. I promised faithfully I would say nothing to my grandmother of what she told me but she wouldn't trust me, and I dare say she was right. But it was very tantalizing because what there was to know, Evie knew. She knew everything, as much as my grandparents did. She even knew who the letters were from but she would never say. My grandmother was capable of throwing her out.

"She wanted to throw your mother out," said Mrs. Poulter. "Before you were born, I mean. I suppose I shouldn't be telling you this at your age, but you've got to know sometime. It was Evie stopped her. Well, that's what they say. Though how she did it when she never stands up for herself I wouldn't know."

Basenjis are barkless dogs. They can learn to bark if they are kept with other sorts of dogs, but left to themselves they never do, though they squeak a bit and make grunting sounds. Basenjis are clean and gentle, and it is a libel to say they are bad-tempered. They are an ancient breed of hound dog native to central Africa, where they are used to point and retrieve and drive quarry into a net. Since I left that house I have always had a basenji of my own, and now

I have two. What could be more natural than that I should love above all other objects of affection the kind I first loved?

My grandparents were not fond of animals, and Evie was allowed to keep the basenji only because he did not bark. I am sure my grandmother must have put him through some kind of barking test before she admitted him to the house. Evie and the basenji had a section of the house to live in by themselves. If this sounds like uncharacteristic generosity on my grandmother's part—you will not expect this from her after what I have said—in fact their rooms were two north-facing attics, the back stairs, and what Mrs. Poulter called the old scullery. All the time I was not at school (taken there and fetched by Evie in the old Morris Minor Estate car), I spent with her and the basenji in the old scullery. And in the summer, when the evenings were light, I took the basenji for his walks.

You will have been wondering why I made no attempt to examine those scrap-books or read those letters. Why did I never go into the sewing-room in my grandmother's absence or penetrate my grandfather's study in the daytime? I tried. Though my grandmother seldom went out, she seemed to me to have an almost supernatural ability to be in two places, or more than two places, at once. She was a very tall, thin woman with a long, narrow face and dark, flat, rather oily hair, which looked as if it were painted on rather than grew. I swear I have stood at the top of the first flight of stairs and seen her at the dining-table that could seat twelve, the scissors in her hand, her head turned as she heard the sound of my breathing; have run down and caught her just inside the drawing-room door, one long dark bony hand on the brass knob;

twisted away swiftly and glimpsed her in the library, taking from the shelves a book destined for mutilation.

It was all my fancy, no doubt. But she was ever-alert, keeping watch. For what? To prevent my discovery of her secrets? She was a mistress of the art of secrecy. I think she loved it for its own sake. At mealtimes she locked the sewing-room door. Perhaps she hung the key around her neck. Certainly she always wore a long chain, though what was on the end of it I never saw, for it was tucked into the vee of her dark dress. The study was never locked up, but all the papers inside it were. One day, from the doorway, I saw the safe. I saw my grandfather take down the painting of an old man in a red coat and with a wig, and move this way and that a dial in the wall behind it.

On Fridays Evie put all the week's newspapers out for the dustmen. She took them out of the drawing-room and brought them downstairs, a sizeable pile which I sometimes went through in the hope of finding clues. Windows had been cut out of most of them, sometimes from the sports pages, sometimes from the arts section, from the home news and the foreign news. Once, in possession of a mutilated copy of the *Times*, I managed, by great guile and considerable labour, to persuade Mrs. Poulter to bring me an identical undamaged copy, which she helped herself to from another house where she cleaned. But the cut-out pieces had been only a report of a tennis tournament and a photograph of a new kind of camellia exhibited at the Chelsea Flower Show.

You might think my grandparents would have wanted to send me to boarding-school as soon as I was old enough to go. They didn't. I would have liked to go away to school, I would have liked to go away anywhere, but Mrs. Poulter said they couldn't afford the fees. That house cost a lot to keep up. Evie went on driving me to school, four miles to the grammar school and back in the morning, and four miles in and four miles back in the afternoon. She must have been in her seventies by then. She always brought the basenji with her in the back of the car, for although she might have left him alone in that house, she would never quite risk leaving him with my grandmother.

I used to badger and badger her about my mother but she would never answer. She told me frankly that she dared not answer. But at last, driven mad by my pestering, she must have said something to my grandmother, for one morning at the breakfast table, after my grandfather had left, after I had brought the post in, including one of the letters in the blue envelopes, my grandmother turned to face me in a slow, portentous way. Her tone remote, she said, "These letters which you have been so curious about for years come from a friend of mine I was at school with. Her handwriting is rather immature, don't you think?"

I think I blushed. I said quite feverishly, "Tell me about my mother."

The tone didn't change nor the look. "Her name is Alexandra. I seldom hear anything of her. I believe she has married."

"Why didn't she have me adopted?" I said. "Why didn't you?"

"Naturally I can't answer for her. I doubt if she ever knew what she was doing. I would have had you adopted if it had been in my power. The mother's consent is needed in these matters."

"Why didn't she want me? Why did she go away?"

"I shan't answer any more questions," my grandmother said. "It would take too long and I should upset myself. You'll know one day. When we're dead and gone, you'll know. All about your mother and what little is known of your father; about the murder, if it was murder; and everything else. And you can tell Evie from me that if she gives you any information about what is no business whatsoever of hers, I shan't see it my duty to give her or that dog of hers house-room any longer."

I passed this message on to Evie. What else could I do? My grandmother always meant what she said, she was a fearful woman, a cold force to be reckoned with. But the murder—what was the murder? In the ten years before I was born, there had been two in the part of the country where we lived. A woman had killed her husband and then herself. A young man, not a local, had been found dead at the wheel of his car, which was parked at the edge of a wood. He had been shot through the head. They never found who did it. I didn't have to ask Mrs. Poulter about these things, they were common knowledge, but I did ask her what they had to do with us.

"They weren't even near here, pet," she said. "The woman who killed her husband and gassed herself, she'd only been living in her house six months. And that young fellow—what was he called? Wilson? Williams?—he drove here from London; he was a stranger."

She was more easily able to explain what my grandmother had meant when she said I would know everything one day, when they were dead and gone.

"They're going to leave you this house and its contents. I know it for a fact. He got me in there to be a witness to their will."

"But they don't even like me," I said.

"You're their flesh and blood. They like you as much as they like anyone, pet. Anyway, it's no big deal, is it? Who'd want it? Great white elephant, it's not worth much."

Not then, perhaps, not then.

When I was fifteen and the basenji was twelve and Evie getting on for eighty, my grandfather went out into the wood with his gun one morning and shot himself. They said it was an accident. After the funeral my grandmother got a carpenter in from London and had him build her three cupboards in the sewing-room. She had the kind of doors put on them that security firms recommend nowadays for the front doors of London flats, reinforced with steel and with locks that when turned caused metal rods to bolt into the door-frame. Into these cupboards she placed the contents of my grandfather's wall safe and all the documents that were in his study. She probably put her own completed scrap-books in there too, for I never saw her at work with scissors and paste again, and there was no more mutilation of books.

There were rumours, and more than rumours, that my grandfather had been in some kind of trouble. Converting his clients' money to his own use or persuading elderly women to make wills in his favour—something of that sort. I suppose that when he went out into the wood that morning it was because he was afraid of criminal proceedings. His death must have averted that. His secrets were in the papers my grandmother hid away. She changed after he was dead, becoming even more cold and remote, and the few acquaintances she had used to see, she shunned. It was a cold house, though she had never seemed to feel it. She did then. Evie began lighting a fire in the grate, and for some reason unknown to me it was my grandfather's cigarette lighter she used to light it, a silver object in the shape of an Aladdin's lamp that stood in the centre of the mantelpiece. For a while my grandmother continued to leave the sewing-room door open and when I passed and looked in, the fire would be alight and she would be writing. She was always writing. Memoirs? A diary? A novel?

Records of births, marriages, and deaths were kept at Somerset House then. When I reached the age my mother was when I was born I went by train to London and looked her up in the appropriate great tome. Alexandra was her name, as my grandmother had said (she never told lies) and she had married, as she also said, a man called Jeremy Harper-Green. They had two children, the Harper-Greens, a boy of six and a girl of four. I think it was when I saw this that I understood I would never meet my mother now.

The basenji was the first to die. He was fifteen and he had had a good life. Evie and I buried him at the bottom of the garden, which was on the side of a hill and from which you could look across the beautiful countryside of Derbyshire and see in the distance the landscape Capability Brown made at Chatsworth. It was winter, the woods dark and the hillsides covered in snow. I dug the grave but Evie was there with me in the intense cold, the biting wind. She caught a cold that night that turned to pneumonia, and a week later she was dead too.

There was nothing to keep me after that. I packed up everything I owned into two suitcases and went to the sewing-room and knocked on the door. For the past year my grandmother had kept that door closed.

She said, "Who is it?" not "Come in," though it could only have been me or a ghost, for Evie was dead and she had given Mrs. Poulter the sack six months before for what she called "filling the child's head with lies and scandals."

I told her I was leaving, I was going to London. She didn't ask me if I had any money, so I was spared telling her that I had taken all the money I found hidden in Evie's rooms, in old handbags and stuffed into vases and wrapped in a scarf at the back of a drawer. Evie had told me often enough she wanted me to have what she left behind. My grandmother didn't ask me but she did me the one good service I ever remember receiving from her hands. She gave me the name and address of that old school friend, the one who wrote the letters in the blue envelopes and who was part-owner of an employment agency in the Strand.

After that she shook hands with me as if I were a caller who had dropped in for half an hour. She didn't get out of her chair. She shook her head in a rueful way and said, not to me but as if there were someone else standing in the doorway to hear her, "Who would have thought it would go on for eighteen years?" Then she picked up her pen and turned back to whatever it was she was writing.

That was nearly thirty years ago. The friend with the employment agency got me a job. I stayed with her until I found a room of my own. I have prospered. I am managing director of my own company now, and if I am not rich, I am comfortably off. My marriage lasted only a short time but there is nothing very unusual in that. Children I never wanted and I have none. Five basenjis have been my companions through the years: one who lived to be twelve, a pair who reached ten and eleven years, respectively, and the fire-year-olds that are with me now. They have been more to me than lovers or children.

Mrs. Poulter told me my grandparents had be-queathed the house to me in their will. The chance of this inheritance I believed I lost forever on the day I left, closed the sewing-room door behind me and went down the stairs to the front door. I never heard from my grandmother again, wrote no letters and received none. By then, for she was something over sixty when I went, I believed she was very likely dead. I seldom thought of her. I have worked hard at blocking off the misery of my early years.

The solicitor's letter coming one Monday morning four years ago told me she had died and left me the house. The funeral had taken place. I wondered who had seen to the arrangements. The Harper-Greens? If they expected a legacy they were disappointed, for it all came to me, the house and everything in it, the grounds from which you could see the sweeping meadows and the woods of Chatsworth.

Now I should know the answers to all those questions, the solutions to many mysteries. I drove up there one morning in autumn, my basenjis, who were puppies then, with me in the back of the estate car. Was the truth that she had loved me all along, valued me in her cold, inexpressive way? Or had she simply not bothered to change the will because, though she cared nothing for me, there was no one else she cared more for? I inclined towards this view. As I drove through the shires and the dukeries, the keys to the house beside me on the passenger seat, I allowed myself to speculate about those things I had long forbidden myself to think of, my grandparents' strange loveless marriage, my mother's refusal to have me adopted, yet willingness to abandon me to a fate she had already experienced, the identity of my father. Which of those murdered men was he? Or was he neither? What then was my family's connection with a murder? What retribution would have caught up with my grandfather if he had waited and faced it instead of going out into the woods with his gun?

We let ourselves into the house, the dogs and I. It was dusty and the ceilings hung with cobwebs, but the smell that met me as I walked up the stairs was the smell of paper, old paper turned yellow with time and packed away in airless places. The sewing-room door was not locked. There were ashes in the grate and the silver Aladdin's lamp lighter was still on the mantelpiece. A sheet of paper lay on the blotter on the table that was big enough to seat twelve. There were nine or ten lines of writing on it, the final sentence broken off in the middle, a fountain pen lying where my grandmother had dropped it and a splutter of ink trailing from the last, half-completed word. It was a kind of awe I felt and a growing dismay. The miseries I thought I had succeeded in forgetting began to crowd back and those earliest memories.

With the keys from the bunch I held I unlocked the burglar-proof cupboard doors. It was all there, all the secrets—in fifty scrap-books, in a thousand letters received and a thousand copies of letters sent, in a hundred diaries, in deeds and agreements and contracts, in unnumbered handwritten manuscripts. The smell of paper, or perhaps it was the smell of ink, was acrid and nauseating. The dogs padded about the room, sniffing in corners, sniffing along skirting-boards and around chair legs, sniffing and holding up their heads as if in thought, as if considering what it was they had smelt.

I began emptying the cupboards. Everything would have to be examined page by page, word by word, and in this house, in this room. How could I take it away except in a removal van? I imagined the misery of it, the enclosing oppression as sad and dreadful things were slowly revealed. The tears came into my eyes and I began to weep as I knelt there on the floor with the piles of paper all round me. The dogs came and licked my hands as dogs licked the sores of Lazarus.

Presently I got up and went to the fireplace and took my grandfather's silver lighter off the mantelpiece. I struck it with my thumb and the flame flared orange and blue. The basenjis were watching me. They watched me as I applied the lighter to the pile of paper and the flame began to lick across the first sheet, lick, die, smoulder, lick, crackle, burst into bright flame.

I picked up the dogs, one under each arm, and ran down the stairs. The front door slammed behind me. What happened to the keys I don't know, I think I left them inside. I didn't look back but drove fast away and back to London.

The house had been insured but of course I didn't claim on the insurance. The land belongs to me and I could have another house built on it, but I don't suppose I ever shall. Two years ago a tour company wrote to me and asked if they might bring parties to look at the burnt-out shell as part of a scenic Derbyshire round trip. So now, I am told, the coach that goes to Chatsworth and Haddon Hall and Bess of Hardwick's house follows the winding road up the hill to my childhood home and shows off to tourists the blackened ruin and the incomparable view.

I will never forget the way the police told me my house had burnt down. Later they hinted at arson, and this is how the guide explains the destruction to visitors. But that same evening, when I had only been back a few hours, the police came and spoke to me very gently and carefully. I must sit down, keep calm, prepare myself for something very upsetting.

They called it bad news.

Mother's Help

1

The little boy would be three at the end of the year. He was big for his age. Nell, who was his nanny but who modestly called herself a mother's help, was perturbed by his inability, or unwillingness, to speak. It was very likely no more than unwillingness, for Daniel was not deaf, that was apparent, and the doctor who carried out tests on him said he was intelligent. His parents and Nell knew that without being told.

He was inordinately fond of motor vehicles. No one knew why, since neither Ivan nor Charlotte took any particular interest in cars. They had one, of course, and both drove it, but Charlotte confessed that she had never understood the workings of the internal-combustion engine. Their son's passion amused them. When he woke up in the morning he got into bed with them and ran toy trucks and miniature tractors over the pillows, shouting, "Brrm, brrm, brrm."

"Say 'car,' Daniel," said Charlotte. "Say 'lorry.'"

"Brrm, brrm, brrm," said Daniel.

One of the things he liked to do was sit in the driver's seat on Ivan's knee or Charlotte's and, strictly supervised, pull the levers and buttons that worked the windscreen wipers, the lights, put the automatic transmission into "drive," make the light come on that flashed when the passenger failed to wear a seat-belt, lift off the hand-brake, and, naturally, sound the horn. All the time he was doing these things he was saying, "Brrm, brrm, brrm." The summer before he was three he said "car" and "tractor" and "engine" as well as "brrm, brrm, brrm." He had been able to say "Mummy" and "Daddy" and "Nell" for quite a long time. Soon his vocabulary grew large and Nell stopped worrying, though Daniel made no attempt to form sentences.

"It may be because he's an only child," she said to Ivan one evening when she came down from putting Daniel to bed.

"And likely to remain one," said Ivan, "in the circumstances."

He kept his voice low. Charlotte had stayed late at work but she was home now, taking off her raincoat in the hall. Because Charlotte was there, Nell made no reply to this cryptic remark of Ivan's. She tried to smile in a reproachful way but failed. Charlotte went upstairs to say good night to Daniel, and in a little while Ivan went up too. Alone, Nell thought how handsome Ivan was and how there was something very masterful, not to say ruthless, about him. The idea of Ivan's ruthlessness made her feel quite excited. Charlotte was the sort of woman people called "attractive," without meaning that they, or any others in particular, were attracted by her. Nell guessed that she was quite a lot older than Ivan, or perhaps she just looked older.

"I wish I'd met you four years ago," Ivan said one afternoon when Charlotte was at work and he had taken the day off. He had been married nearly four years. Nell had seen the cards he and Charlotte got for their third wedding anniversary.

"I was only seventeen then," she said. "I was still at school."

"What difference does that make?"

Daniel was pushing a miniature Land Rover along the windowsill and along the skirting-board and up the side of the door-frame, saying, "Brrm, brrm." He got up onto a chair, fell off and started screaming. Nell picked him up and held him in her arms.

"You look so lovely," said Ivan. "You look like a Murillo madonna."

Ivan was the owner of a picture gallery in Mayfair and knowledgeable about things like that. He asked Nell if it wasn't time for Daniel's sleep but Nell said he was getting too old to sleep in the daytime and she usually took him out for a walk. "I shall come with you," said Ivan.

It was August and business was slack—though not Charlotte's business—and Ivan began taking days off more often. He told Charlotte he liked to be with Daniel as much as possible. Unless they were put to bed at some ridiculously late hour of the night, children grew up hardly knowing their fathers.

"Or their mothers," said Charlotte.

"No one obliges you to work."

"That's true. I'm thinking of giving up and then we wouldn't need to keep Nell on."

Nell couldn't drive. When she went shopping, Ivan drove her. He came home specially early to do this. The house was a detached Victorian villa and the garage a converted coach-house with a door that pulled down, rather like a roller blind. When the car had been backed out, it was tiresome to have to get out and pull down the door, but leaving the garage open was, as Charlotte said, an invitation to burglars. Nell sat in the front, in the passenger seat, and Daniel in the back. In those days, safety-belts in the rear of cars had scarcely been thought of, and child-seats were unusual.

It happened very suddenly. Ivan left the car in "park" and the hand-brake on and went to close the garage door. Fortunately for him, he noticed a pool of what seemed to be oil at the back of the garage on the concrete floor and took a step or two inside to investigate. Daniel, with a shout of "Brrm, brrm!" but without any other warning, lunged forward across the top of the driver's seat and made a grab for all the controls. He flipped on the lights, made the full beam blaze, whipped the transmission into "drive," sent sprays of water across the windscreen, and tugged off the hand-brake.

The car shot forward with blazing lights. Nell screamed. She didn't know how to stop it, she didn't know what the hand-brake was, where the foot-brake was, she could only seize hold of laughing triumphant Daniel. The car, descending the few feet of slope, charged into the garage, slowing as it met level ground, sliding to a stop while Ivan stood on tiptoe, flattening himself against the wall.

Nell began to cry. She was very frightened. Seeing

Ivan in danger made her understand all kinds of things about herself and him she hadn't realized before. He came out and switched off the engine and carried Daniel back into the house. Nell followed, still crying. Ivan took her in his arms and kissed her. Her knees felt weak and she thought she might faint, from shock perhaps or perhaps not. Ivan forced her lips apart with his tongue and put his tongue in her mouth and said after a moment or two that they should go upstairs. "Not with Daniel in the house," Nell moaned.

"Daniel is always in the bloody house," said Ivan.

When Charlotte came home they told her what Daniel had done. They didn't feel like talking, especially to Charlotte, but it would have looked unnatural to say nothing. Charlotte said Ivan should speak to Daniel, he should speak to him very gently but very firmly too, and explain to him that what he had done was extremely naughty. It was dangerous and might have hurt Daddy. So Ivan took Daniel on his knee and gave him a lecture in a kind but serious way, impressing on him that he must never again do what he had done that afternoon.

"Daniel drive car," said Daniel.

It was the first sentence any of them had heard him speak, and Charlotte, in spite of the seriousness of the occasion, was enraptured. They thought it wiser to tell no one else about what had happened, but this resolve was quickly broken. Charlotte told her mother and her mother-in-law, and Nell confessed to Charlotte that she had told her boy-friend. Nell didn't in fact have a boy-friend, but she wanted Charlotte to think she had. Their doctor and his wife came to dinner and they told them. Ivan knew he had repeated the story to the doctor (and the four other guests at the table) because it was an example of the intelligence of a child some people might otherwise be starting to think of as backward. When an opportunity arose, he told the two women who worked for him at the gallery, and Charlotte told her boss and the girl who did her typing.

In September Charlotte took two weeks holiday. Business hadn't yet picked up at the gallery and they could have gone away somewhere, but that would have meant taking Nell with them and Charlotte didn't want to pay some extortionate hotel bill for her as well. She was going to stay at home with her son and Nell could have the afternoons off. Charlotte's mother had said that in her opinion Nell was stealing Daniel's affections in an indefensible way. Ivan took Nell to a motel on the A.12 where he pretended they were a married couple on their way to Harwich en route for a weekend in Amsterdam.

Nell had been nervous about this aspect of things at first, but now she was so much in love with Ivan that she wanted him to be making love to her all the time. Every time she saw him, which was for hours of every day, she wanted him to be making love to her.

"I shall have to think what's to be done," said Ivan in the motel room. "We can't just go off together."

"Oh, no, I see that. You'd lose your little boy."

"I'd lose my house and half my income," said Ivan.

They got home very late, Ivan coming in first, Nell half an hour later by pre-arrangement. Ivan told Charlotte he had been working until eleven getting ready for a private view. She wasn't sure that she believed him but she believed Nell when Nell said she had been to the cinema with her boy-friend. Nell was always out with this boy-friend, it was evidently serious, and Charlotte wasn't sorry. Nell would get married, and married women don't remain as live-in mother's helps. If Nell left, she wouldn't have to sack her. She was having strange feelings about Nell, though she couldn't exactly define what they were, perhaps no more than fear of Daniel's preferring the mother's help to herself.

"He'll go to her before he goes to you," said Charlotte's mother. "You want to watch that."

He was always on Nell's lap, hugging her. He liked her to bathe him. It was Nell who was favoured when a bedtime story was to be read, sweet-faced Nell with the soft blue eyes and the long fair hair. He seemed particularly to like the touch of her slim fingers and to press himself close against her. One Saturday morning when Nell was cutting up vegetables for his lunch, Daniel ran up behind her and threw his arms round her legs. Nell hadn't heard him coming, the knife slipped and she cut her left hand in a long gash across the forefinger and palm.

2

The cut extended from the first joint of the forefinger diagonally across to the wrist, following the course of what palmists call the lifeline. The sight of blood, especially her own, upset Nell. She had given one loud cry and now she was making frightened whimpering sounds. Blood was pouring out of her hand, spouting out in little leaps like an oil well she had seen on television. It dripped off the edge of the counter, and Daniel, who wasn't at all upset by the sight of it, caught the drips on his forefinger and drew squiggles on the cupboard door.

Charlotte, coming into the kitchen, guessed what had happened and was cross. If Nell hadn't encouraged Daniel in these displays of affection, he wouldn't have hugged her like that and she wouldn't have cut herself. He should have been outside in the fresh air hugging his mother, who had a trowel, not a knife, in her hand. Charlotte had been looking forward to an early lunch so that she could spend the afternoon planting twelve Little Pet roses in the circular bed in the front garden.

"You'll have to have that stitched," she said. "You'll have to have an anti-tetanus injection." What Daniel was doing registered with her and she pulled him away. "That's very naughty and disgusting, Daniel!" Daniel began to scream and punch at Charlotte with his fists.

"Shall I have to go to hospital?" said Nell.

"Of course you will. We'll get that tied up, we'll have to try and stop the bleeding." Ivan was in the house, upstairs in the room he called his study. It would be more convenient for Charlotte if she could get Ivan to drive Nell to the hospital, but unaccountably she felt a sudden strong dislike of this idea. It hadn't occurred to her before, but she didn't want to leave Ivan alone with Nell again. "I'll drive you. We'll take Daniel with us."

"Couldn't we leave him with Ivan?" said Nell, who had wrapped a tea-cloth tightly round her hand and was watching the blood work its way through the pattern, which was a map of Scotland. "We could tell

Ivan and ask him to look after Daniel. Perhaps," she added hopefully, "we won't be very long."

"I'd appreciate it if you didn't interfere with my arrangements," said Charlotte very sharply.

Nell started crying. Daniel, who was still crying into Charlotte's shoulder, reached out his arms to her. With an exclamation of impatience, Charlotte handed him over. She washed the earth off her hands at the kitchen sink while Nell sniffled and crooned over Daniel. They took coats from the rack in the hall, Charlotte happening to grab an olive-green padded jacket her mother-in-law had left behind, and went out through the front door. The twelve roses lay in a line along the edge of the flower-bed, their roots wrapped up in green plastic. Nell stood on the garage drive cuddling Daniel, the tea-cloth not providing a very effective bandage. Blood had now entirely obscured Caithness and Sutherland. Looking down at it, Nell began to feel faint, and it was quite a different sort of faintness from the way she felt when Ivan started kissing her.

Charlotte raised the garage door, got into the car and backed it out. She took Daniel from Nell and put him on the back seat, where he kept a fleet of small motor vehicles, trucks and tanks and saloon cars. Already regretting that she had spoken so harshly to Nell, she opened the passenger door for her. Pale, pretty Nell, in a very becoming thin black raincoat, had grown fragile from shock and pain.

"You'd better sit down. Put your head back and close your eyes. You're as white as a sheet."

"Brrm, brrm," said Daniel, running a Triumph Dolomite up the back of the driver's seat.

Since Ivan was in the house, there was no need to

close the garage door. It occurred to Charlotte that, antagonistic towards him though she felt, she had better tell him they were going out and where they were going. But before she reached the front door, it opened and Ivan came out.

"What's happened? Why was everyone yelling?"

She told him. He said, "I shall drive Nell to hospital. Naturally, I want to drive her, I should have thought you'd know that. I can't understand why you didn't come and tell me as soon as this happened."

Charlotte said nothing. She was thinking. She seemed to hear in Ivan's voice a note of unusual concern, the kind of care a man might show for someone close and dear to him. And, incongruously, that look of his that had originally attracted her to him had returned. More than ever he resembled some brigand or pirate who required for perfect conviction only a pair of gold earrings or a knife between his teeth.

"There's absolutely no need for you to go," he said in the rough way he had lately got into the habit of using to her. "It's pointless a great crowd of us going."

Putting two and two together, seeing all kinds of things fall delicately into place, recalling lonely evenings and bizarre excuses, Charlotte said, "I am certainly going. I am going to that hospital if it's the last thing I do."

"Suit yourself."

Ivan got into the driving seat. He said to Nell, "Bear up, sweetheart. What a bloody awful thing to happen."

Nell opened her eyes and gave him a wan smile, pushing back with her good hand the curtain of daffodil-coloured hair that had fallen across her pale, tearful face. In the back, Daniel put his arms round his father's neck from behind and ran the Triumph Dolomite up the lapels of his jacket.

"The least you could do is close the garage door," Charlotte shouted. "That's all we need, to come back and find someone's been in and nicked the stereo."

Ivan didn't move. He was looking at Nell. Charlotte walked down the drive to the garage door. With her back to the bonnet of the car, she reached up for the recessed handle in the door to pull it down. The green padded jacket went badly with her blue cord trousers and it made her look fat.

His hands on the steering wheel, Ivan turned slowly to look at her. Daniel was hanging on to his neck now, pushing the toy car up under Ivan's chin. "Brrm, brrm, brrm!"

"Stop that, Daniel, please. Don't do that."

"Drive car," said Daniel.

"All right," said Ivan. "Why not?"

He put the transmission into "drive," all the lights on, set the windscreen jets spouting, the wipers going, took off the hand-brake, and stamped his foot hard onto the accelerator. As the car plunged forward, Charlotte, who had pulled the door down to its fullest extent and was still bending over, sprang up, alerted by the blaze of light. She gave a loud scream, flinging out her hands as if to hold back the car. In that moment Nell, her eyes jerked open, her body propelled forward almost against the windscreen, saw Charlotte's face as if both their faces had swung to meet each other. Charlotte's face seemed to loom and grimace like a bogey in a ghost tunnel. It was a sight Nell was never to forget: Charlotte's expression of horror, and the knowledge that was also there, the awareness of why.

The weak hands, the desperate arms were ineffectual against the juggernaut propulsion of the big car. Charlotte fell backwards, crying out, screaming. The bonnet obscured her fall, the wheels went over her, as the car burst through the garage door, which against this onslaught was as flimsy as a roller blind.

Fragments of shattered door fell all over the bonnet and roof of the car. A triangular-shaped slice of it split the windscreen and turned it into a sheet of frosted glass. Nell was jumping up and down in her seat, making hysterical shrieks, but on the back seat Daniel, who had retreated into the corner behind his father, was silent, holding a piece of the hem of his coat in his fingers and pushing it into his mouth.

Blinded by the whitening and cobwebbing of the glass, Ivan recoiled from it, put his foot on the brake and pulled on the hand-brake. The car emitted a deep musical note, like a rich chord drawn from a church organ, as it sometimes did when brought to a sudden stop. Ivan lifted his hands from the wheel, tossed his head as if to shake back a fallen lock of hair, and rested against the seat, closing his eyes. He breathed deeply and steadily, like someone about to fall asleep.

"Ivan," screamed Nell, "Ivan, Ivan, Ivan!"

He turned his head with infinite slowness, and when it was fully turned to face her, opened his eyes. Meeting his eyes had the immediate effect of silencing her. She whimpered. He put out his hand and touched the side of her cheek, not with his fingertips, but very gently with his knuckles. He ran his knuckles along the line of her jaw and the curve of her neck.

"Your hand has stopped bleeding," he said in a whisper.

She looked down at the bundle in her lap, a red

sodden mass. She didn't know why he said that or what he meant. "Oh, Ivan, Ivan, is she dead? She must be dead—is she?"

"I'm going to get you back into the house."

"I don't want to go into the house, I want to die; I just want to give up and die!"

"Yes, well, on second thoughts it might be best for you to stay where you are. Just for a while. And Daniel too. I shall go and phone the police."

She got hold of him as he tried to get out. She got hold of his jacket and held on, weeping. "Oh, Ivan, Ivan, what have you done?"

"Don't you mean," he said, "what has Daniel done?"

3

When he came back from his investigations underneath the car, Ivan knelt on the driver's seat. He brought his face very close to hers. "I'm going back into the house. I was in the house when it happened. I came running out when I heard the crash and as soon as I saw what had happened I went back in to call the police and an ambulance."

"I don't understand what you mean," said Nell.

"Yes, you do. Think about it. I was upstairs in my study. You were alone in the car with Daniel, resting your head back with your eyes closed."

"Oh, no, Ivan, no. I couldn't say that, I couldn't tell people that."

"You needn't tell them anything. You can be in a

53

state of shock, you are in a state of shock. Telling people things will come later. You'll be fine by then."

Nell put her hands up to her face, her right hand and the bandaged one. She peered out between her fingers like a child that has had a fright. "Is she—is she dead?"

"Oh, yes, she's dead," said Ivan.

"Oh my God, my God, and she said she was coming to the hospital if it was the last thing she did!"

"Closing the garage door was the last thing she did."

He went into the house. Nell started crying again. She sobbed, she hung her head and threw it back against the seat and howled. She had completely forgotten Daniel. He sat on the back seat munching on the hem of his coat, his fleet of motor vehicles ignored. The people next door, who had been eating their lunch when they heard the noise of the car going through the garage door, came down the drive to see what was the matter. They were joined by the man from a Gas Board van and a girl who had been distributing leaflets advertising double glazing. It was a dull, grey day, and the front gardens here were planted with tall trees and thick evergreen shrubs. Trees grew in the pavements. No one had seen the car go over Charlotte and through the garage door, no one had seen who was driving.

The people next door were helping Nell out of the car when Ivan emerged from the front door. Nell saw one of Charlotte's feet sticking out from under the car and Charlotte's blood on the concrete of the drive and the scattered bits of door and began screaming again. The woman from next door smacked her face. Her husband, conveniently doing the best part of Ivan's work for him, said, "What an appalling thing, what a ghastly tragedy. Who would have thought the poor little chap would get up to his tricks again with such tragic results?"

"Don't look at it, dear," said the double-glazing girl, making a screen out of her leaflets between Nell and the body, which lay half outside and half under the car. "Let's get you indoors."

Nell gave another wail when she saw the Little Pet roses all lying there waiting to be planted. The woman next door went into Charlotte's kitchen to make a cup of tea and her husband came in carrying Daniel who, when he saw Nell, spoke another sentence of sorts.

"Daniel hungry."

"I'll see to him, I'll find something for him," said the woman next door, dispensing tea. "Bring him out here, poor little mite. He's not to blame, the little innocent; how was he to know?"

"You see," said Ivan when they were alone.

"You can't mean to tell people Daniel did it. You can't, Ivan."

"I can't, agreed, but you can. I wasn't there. I was up in my study."

"Ivan, the police will come and ask me."

"That's right, and there'll be an inquest, certain to be. The coroner will ask you and police will probably ask you again and maybe solicitors will ask you, I don't know, a lot of different people, but they'll be kind to you, they'll be understanding."

"I can't tell lies to people like that, Ivan."

"Yes, you can, you're a very good liar. Remember all those lies you told to Charlotte. She believed you. Remember that boy-friend you invented and all the times you said you'd been to the cinema with him when you'd been with me? Besides, you don't have to lie. You only have to tell them what happened last time, only this time poor old Charlotte got in the way."

Nell burst into sobs. "Oh, I can't stop crying, I can't. What shall I do?"

"You don't have to stop crying. It's probably a very good thing for you to cry quite a lot. Now don't stop crying but listen to me if you can. Daniel can't tell them because Daniel can't speak so's you'd notice. And it doesn't matter anyway because no one's going to blame him. You heard what Mrs. Whatever-Her-Name-Is said about no one blaming him, the little innocent, how was he to know? Children aren't supposed to know what they're doing before they're seven, before the age of reason. Everyone is well aware of what Daniel gets up to in cars, everyone knows he did it before."

"But he didn't do it this time."

"Never say that again. Don't even think it. Everyone will assume it was Daniel and you will only have to confirm it."

"I don't think I can, Ivan; I don't think I can face it."

"You know what will happen to me if you can't face it, don't you?"

The police came before Nell had time to answer.

It was something of a dilemma for them because Daniel was so young, but he helped them by coming into the room where they were interviewing his father and confirming, so to speak, what Ivan had told them.

"Daniel drive."

They exchanged glances with Ivan and Nell and one of them wrote Daniel's words down. It was as if, Nell thought, they were taking down what he said to use it in evidence at his trial, only Daniel, naturally, wouldn't have a trial. He sat on her lap, holding one of his cars in his hand, but in silence. Nell said afterwards to Ivan that from that day forwards he never said "Brrm, brrm," again, but neither of them could be sure of this. When it was time for the police to go, they took Nell with them to the hospital, where at last she had her hand cleaned and the wound stitched. The sister in Out-Patients, who didn't know the circumstances, said it was a pity she hadn't come as soon as it had happened, for now she would probably be scarred for life.

"I expect I shall," said Nell.

"There's always plastic surgery," the sister said in a cheerful way.

By the time the inquest took place, the car had been fitted with a new windscreen and was scheduled for a re-spray, the garage had been measured for a new door, and Daniel had learned to utter several more sentences. But those who had power in these matters, a doctor or two and the coroner and the coroner's officer, all agreed that it would be unwise from a psychological point of view to mention again in his hearing the events of that Saturday morning. Not, at least, until he was quite a lot older. It would be better not to attempt any questioning of him, and admonition at this stage seemed useless. The wisest course, the coroner said when the inquest was almost over, was for his father to ensure that Daniel never again sat in the back of a car on his own unless he was strapped in or closely supervised.

Nell gave her evidence in a low, subdued voice. Several times she had to be asked to speak more loudly. She described how she had sat in the car, feeling faint, her eyes closed. There was no one in the driver's seat, Charlotte had gone to close the garage door, when suddenly Daniel, shouting, "Brrm, brrm," had precipitated himself forwards and, seizing the controls, switched on the lights, flashed up the full beam, pushed the transmission into "drive," set the water jets spraying across the windscreen, taken off the handbrake. No, it wasn't the first time he had done it, he had done it once before, only that time his mother hadn't been in the path of the car, bending down to close the garage door.

The coroner asked her if she had attempted to stop the child but Nell burst into tears at this and, in a gesture that seemed dramatic but was in fact involuntary, held out, palm-upwards, her wounded hand, at that time still thickly bandaged. She often found herself staring at that hand in the weeks, the months, the years to come, at the white scar that bisected it from the first joint of the forefinger to the fleshy pad that cushioned out at the point where hand met wrist. She looked at it when she held her third finger up for Ivan to put the wedding ring on.

"Death by misadventure" the verdict had been, "misadventure," Ivan said, meaning "accident." She had cut her finger by misadventure and she sometimes wondered if any of this would have happened if she hadn't cut it. If, in point of fact, Daniel hadn't run up behind her and thrown his arms round her legs. So perhaps, in a curious way, it really was his fault after all. She said something of this to Ivan, who agreed, but he never mentioned anything about any of it again. Nell never mentioned it either. The event, which he had certainly witnessed, had no apparent ill effects on Daniel. He was four when they got married and talking like any other normal four-year-old. He didn't appear to miss his mother, but then, as Ivan said, he had always preferred Nell.

When Nell's daughter was born after they had been married five years and she had begun to give up hope of ever having a child, Daniel, eyeing the baby Emma, surprised her by asking about his mother. He asked her how Charlotte had died. In a car crash, Nell said, which was the answer she and Ivan had agreed on.

"One day you're going to have to tell him more," said Nell. "What are you going to tell him?"

4

Ivan didn't say anything. His expression was guarded yet calculating. As he got older, the ruthlessness that had helped to give him his dashing piratical appearance now made him look wolfish. Nell repeated her question.

"What are you going to tell Daniel when he asks you how Charlotte died?"

"I shall say in a car crash."

"Well, he's not going to be satisfied with that, is he? He'll want to know details. He'll want to know who was driving and was anyone else involved and all that."

"I shall tell him the truth," said Ivan.

"You can't tell him the truth! How can you possibly? What's he going to think of you if you tell him that? He'll hate your guts. I mean, he may even go and tell people that his father—well, you know. I can't, frankly, bring myself to put it into words."

"I am delighted to hear there is something you can't bring yourself to put into words. It makes a pleasant change." When something riled him Ivan had got into the habit of curling back his upper lip to expose his teeth and his red gums.

"What precisely do you intend to tell Daniel, Ivan?"

"When the occasion arises, I shall tell him the truth about Charlotte's death. I shall tell him that though he was technically responsible for it, he couldn't at his age be blamed. I shall tell him as honestly as I can that he got hold of the controls of the car and drove it into Charlotte."

"And that's the truth?"

"You should know," said Ivan, wolf-faced, his upper lip curling. "That's what you told the inquest."

Daniel had only asked about his mother, Nell thought, because he was jealous. He was jealous of Emma. Until then he had had all Nell's attention, or all the attention she could spare from Ivan. Seeing Nell with this newcomer, understanding perhaps that she would no longer be exclusively his, recalled to him that he had once had a real mother of his own.

There were many things to recall her to Nell. Each time—which was every day—she saw those Little Pet roses, she thought of Charlotte. Ivan had planted them himself, the day after Charlotte's funeral. They never used the car again, that went in part-exchange for a new one. When Emma was a year old, they moved out of the house and into a larger, older one. Nell was happy to be rid of those roses, but she couldn't get rid of her own hand with the white scar across it that followed in that sinister way the path of the lifeline.

And she couldn't avoid occasionally seeing a map of Scotland.

At the new house they lost their baby-sitter. The woman next door had sat for them but wasn't prepared to travel ten miles. Ivan had several times suggested they engage a mother's help, but Nell was against this. She remembered the way Daniel had always seemed to prefer her to his own mother. Besides, since they were married she had never been in what Ivan called gainful employment. She had worked, of course, but this had been at the tiring and time-consuming task of looking after Daniel, and then Emma too. And she had kept the house very clean and beautiful.

A girl who was employed by Ivan at the gallery lived no more than a couple of streets away. She said she loved children and offered to baby-sit for them once a week. Ivan told Nell she was called Denise and was twenty-three but nothing else, and it came as something of a shock to discover that she was also very pretty and had wavy long chestnut hair. In fact, they needed her less frequently than once a week, for Ivan so often worked late that, on the evenings he did come home in time for dinner, he didn't feel like going out again.

"Emma will grow up hardly knowing her father," said Nell.

"Go and be a mother's help then," said Ivan. "If you can earn what I do, I'll be happy to retire and look after the kids."

Denise sat for them on the evening of their sixth wedding anniversary and on Nell's birthday. Emma, whom Nell suspected of being hyperactive, stayed awake most of the time Denise was there, sitting on

Denise's lap, playing with the contents of Denise's handbag, and screaming when attempts were made to put her back to bed. Denise said she didn't mind, she loved children. Emma clung to her and hit out at Nell with her fists when Nell tried to take her out of the girl's arms.

"I'll drive you home," said Nell.

"You don't need to do that," said Ivan. "I'll do that. You stay here with Emma."

Denise had a boy-friend she was always talking about. When she couldn't baby-sit it was because she was going out somewhere with her boy-friend. Ivan said he had seen him come for Denise at the gallery, but when Nell asked what he was like, the best Ivan could do in the way of a description was to say he was just ordinary and nothing in particular. Nell didn't know where they would find another baby-sitter but sometimes she hoped Denise was serious about her boy-friend, because if she was, she might get married and move away.

It was preposterous of Ivan to suggest, even in that satirical way, that Nell might get a job herself. She had her hands full with Emma, who had an abnormal amount of energy for a child of eighteen months. Emma had walked when she was ten months old and never slept for more than six hours a night, though sometimes during the day she would collapse and fall asleep through sheer exhaustion. It wasn't surprising that she hadn't yet uttered a word, she was younger than all that activity made her seem, and as Nell remarked to Daniel, she hadn't got *time* to talk.

"You didn't talk till you were nearly three," said Nell, and, mistakenly, as she quickly realized, "there must be something about your father's children . . ."

"Yes," said Daniel, "there must be. It can't be you or my mother. I'd like to know what happened to my mother."

"It was a car crash."

"Yes, I know. I mean I'd like to know details, I'd like to know exactly what happened."

"Your father will tell you when you're older."

Nell had made a mystery of it and this she knew was an error. She intended to warn Ivan, but for days on end she hardly saw him. They had made an arrangement to go out on the Friday evening, but Ivan phoned to say he was working late and that he would get in touch with Denise and put her off. He got home at midnight and nearly as late on Saturday. Daniel managed to catch him on Sunday morning.

"In some ways, the sooner Daniel goes away to school, the better," Ivan said to Nell.

"That won't be for a year."

"It might be a good idea for him to go as a boarder somewhere for that year."

"I don't want him to go away, I want him to stay here. And it's no good you saying he's not my child, it's nothing to do with me, because he's more mine than yours. You've never liked him."

Ivan's hair, once the black of a raven's wing, had begun to go grey early. It was the colour of a wolf's pelt now and the moustache he had grown was iron-grey. Perhaps it was the contrast this provided that made the inside of his mouth look so red and his teeth so white when he indulged in that ugly mannerism of curling back his upper lip. If he were an animal, Nell's mother said, you would call it a snarl, but men don't snarl.

"Are you saying I don't like my own child?"

"Yes, I am. I am saying that. We don't like the people we've injured, it's a well-known fact."

"What utter nonsense. How am I supposed to have injured Daniel?"

Nell looked down at her left hand. This had become an almost involuntary gesture with her, like a tic. She turned it palm-downwards and put her thumb across the base of her forefinger to hide the scar. "I suppose he asked you about Charlotte?"

"I told him you were the only person who could tell him. You were there and I wasn't. Of course, if you weren't prepared to tell him, I said, that was your decision. I wish you'd have something done about your hand. It doesn't get less unsightly as you get older. They can do marvels with scars these days, and it isn't as if I'd grudge the expense."

It was six months since Denise had baby-sat for them. They didn't need her because they never went out. Or they never went out together. Ivan was always out. Nell stayed at home and looked after Daniel and Emma and kept the house very clean. She had become obsessive about it, her mother said, it wasn't healthy.

One afternoon she was putting the vacuum cleaner away when Emma, who had been running in and out, shut her in the broom cupboard. The cupboard door, which was heavy and solid in that old house, had a handle on the outside but not the inside. Nell, determined not to panic, began cajoling Emma to open the door and release her. "Please, Emma, there's a good girl, open the door, Emma, let Mummy out. . . ."

5

For a little while Emma stood outside the door. Nell could hear her giggling.

"Let Mummy out, Emma. Emma's such a clever girl, she can open the door, but Mummy can't. Mummy's not clever enough to open the door."

Nell thought this flattery and self-abasement might have some effect on Emma. The giggling stopped. Nell waited in the dark. It was pitch-dark in the cupboard, and there wasn't even a line of light round the edge of the door. It fitted into its frame too well for that. The cupboard was in the middle of the house, between an interior wall and the solid brick of the chimney-bay. The air in there was thick and black and it smelt of dust and soot. Emma gave another very light soft giggle. Nell knew why it sounded so soft. Emma was moving away from the door.

"Emma, come back. Come back and let Mummy out. Just turn the handle and the door will open and Mummy can get out."

The little footsteps sounded very light as they retreated. They sounded, too, as if the feet that made them moved not with their customary swiftness but sluggishly. With a sinking of the heart, Nell realized what had happened. This was what often happened to Emma after a long frenzied spell of hyperactivity. She had tired herself out. Seizing her opportunity, Nell would lay Emma down in her cot and cover her up, but what would Emma do in Nell's absence?

Injure herself? Go outside and shut herself out? This was an additional worry. Nell began to hammer on the door with her fists. She began to kick at the door. Not only was she shut up in this cupboard, but her child, her less-than-two-year-old baby, was wandering alone about this big old house of many steps and corners and traps for little children. Emma was tired, Emma was exhausted. Suppose she got the cellar door open and fell down the cellar steps? Suppose she put her fingers into the electricity sockets? Or found matches or knives? Nell couldn't see her hand in the dark but she could feel with the fingers of her other hand the ridge of scar tissue that scored her palm. She hammered on the door and shouted, "Emma, Emma, come back and let Mummy out!"

As well as being black-dark in the cupboard, it was airless. Or Nell imagined it would soon be airless. No air could get in, and once she had used up what oxygen there was—she would die, wouldn't she? She would suffocate. Daniel wouldn't be home for hours; Ivan, to judge by his recent performance, not before midnight. The more she shouted, the more energy she used in beating at the door, the more oxygen her lungs needed.

It was Daniel who rescued her. About an hour after Emma shut Nell in the cupboard, Daniel came home from school. He let himself in and found the house empty, which was most unusual. By that time Nell had stopped shouting and beating on the door. She was sitting on the stone floor with her arms clasped round her knees, keeping very still so as not to exhaust the oxygen in the dusty, sooty air. Daniel wasn't expected home for another hour at least. He should have gone straight to his violin lesson from school, but he had forgotten his music and come home to fetch it.

Although it was almost unknown for Nell to be out when he came home, he knew he wasn't expected home yet. Perhaps she always went out while he was at his violin lesson. With very little time to spare, he would have gone straight up to his bedroom, fetched his music, and gone out again, but as he passed the living-room door he caught a glimpse of pink where no pink should be. This was his sister's pink jump suit. Emma was asleep on the rug in the living-room, her thumb in her mouth, the small brush attachment from the vacuum cleaner lying by her side. The brush provided him with a clue, and as he approached the broom cupboard, Nell heard his footsteps and shouted to him:

"Daniel, Daniel, I'm in here, I'm in the cupboard!"

He released her. Nell staggered out of the cupboard with cobwebs in her hair and blinking her eyes at the light. Daniel seemed rather pleased to see Emma get into trouble, for even after nearly two years he hadn't quite got over his jealousy. He scolded Emma himself and for once Nell didn't stop him.

It was the first evening for weeks that Ivan had come home at a reasonable hour. He had brought Denise with him. They had some unfinished work to get through, and Ivan thought they might as well do it at home. Nell told them of the events of the afternoon and Denise said how clever and enterprising Daniel had been. If he had been less observant, he would have left the house again immediately, and where would poor Nell be now?

"It's hard to see what else he could have done," said Ivan. "You might say with more justice that this is the reverse of virtue rewarded. If Daniel hadn't been so careless as to leave his music behind, he would never have come home when he did. How can you praise someone for that?"

He scowled unpleasantly, but not at Denise. He and Denise would get to work on the new catalogue until eight, and then he would take her out to eat somewhere. They had to have dinner, but there was no need for Nell to cook for them, he said more graciously, especially after her ordeal. Denise said she was terribly pleased Nell was all right. She couldn't wait to see her boy-friend's reaction when she told him the story.

Ivan came in very late. His brown wolf's eyes had a glazed look, sleepy and entranced, a look that Nell had once known very well. Next day she said to him, apropos of nothing in particular, that she thought the day was coming when she would feel obliged to tell Daniel the truth about what had happened to his mother. It might also mean having to tell others and therefore acknowledging that she had committed perjury at the inquest, but she couldn't help that, she would have to face that. Ivan said, didn't she mean *he* would have to face that? And then he said no one would believe her.

"If we split up," Nell said, "I should get custody of these children. Daniel not being my own wouldn't make any difference, I should get custody. But you wouldn't mind that, would you? You don't like children."

"What nonsense. Of course I like children."

"And you'd lose your house and half your income."

"Two-thirds," said Ivan.

"I think you'd like to see the back of Daniel. You can't stand him. And the reason you can't stand him is because one day you know you're either going to have to tell him the truth, which will be the end of you, or tell him a lie that will blight the rest of his life."

"How melodramatic you are," said Ivan, "and how wrong. Anyway, we aren't going to split up, are we?"

"I don't know. I can't go on living like this."

He took Emma on his knee and explained to her how extremely naughty she had been to shut Nell up in the broom cupboard. It was a very dangerous thing to do because there was no air in the cupboard, and people needed air in order to stay alive. Emma squirmed and fidgeted and struggled to get down. When Ivan held her firmly so that she couldn't get away, she bounced up and down on his lap. Suppose Emma herself had come to some harm? asked Ivan who, judging others by himself, hadn't much faith in an appeal to altruism. Suppose she had fallen down the steps and hurt herself?

When Emma had gone to bed, Ivan suggested he and Nell make a fresh start. He would make an effort, he promised, to be home at a reasonable time in the evenings. Dismissing Denise would be tricky, but he thought she would leave of her own accord. And he wouldn't embark on these projects that necessitated working long hours.

"How about Daniel?" said Nell.

Ivan smiled slightly. It was a sad smile, Nell thought. "I'm working out something to tell Daniel." She thought he was looking at the scar on her hand and she turned it palm-downwards. "I shall tell him how it was you sitting in the passenger seat and he was in the back, playing with his cars, and the engine was running. I shall make it plain that he was in no way to blame. Of course I'll explain to him that you were feeling too ill to know what you were doing."

"You needn't make it sound as if I cut myself on purpose. I'm not going to die, you know. I'll be around to answer for myself."

Ivan didn't reply. He said it would be a nice idea to have a party for their seventh wedding anniversary. The people Ivan had known during his first marriage he knew no longer, they had been left behind when he and Nell came to this house. But they invited Nell's mother and Nell's sister and brother-in-law and their doctor and his wife and the neighbours and the woman at the gallery with her husband and the girl who had taken over from Denise. It was a fine moonlit evening for a barbecue and Emma was up and still rushing about the garden at nine, at ten. She was naughty and uncontrollable, Ivan told the doctor, brimming with energy, it was impossible to cope with her.

"Hyperactive, I suppose," said the doctor.

"Exactly," said Ivan. "For example, only a few weeks ago she shut Nell up in a cupboard, closed the door, and just ran off and left her there. If my son hadn't happened to forget something and come back for it, I don't know what would have happened. There's no air in that cupboard." Everyone had stopped talking and was listening to Ivan. Nell, handing round little cheese biscuits, stopped and listened to Ivan. "I gave her a talking-to, you can imagine the kind of thing, but she's only two. Precocious, of course, but basically a baby." Ivan's smile was so wolfish, he looked as if about to lift his head and bay at the moon. "I don't know why it is," he said, "but neither of my children ever do what they're told, they don't listen to a word I say."

Nell dropped the plate and screamed. She stood there screaming until the woman from the gallery went up to her and slapped her face.

LONG LIVE
THE
QUEEN

It was over in an instant. A flash of orange out of the green hedge, a streak across the road, a thud. The impact was felt as a surprisingly heavy jarring. There was no cry. Anna had braked but too late and the car had been going fast. She pulled in to the side of the road, got out, walked back.

An effort was needed before she could look. The cat had been flung against the grass verge that separated road from narrow walkway. It was dead. She knew before she knelt down and felt its side that it was dead. A little blood came from its mouth. Its eyes were already glazing. It had been a fine cat of the kind called marmalade because the colour is two-tone, the stripes like dark slices of peel among the clear orange. Paws, chest, and part of its face were white, the eyes gooseberry-green.

It was an unfamiliar road, one she had only taken to avoid road-works on the bridge. Anna thought, I was going too fast. There is no speed limit here, but it's a country road with cottages, and I shouldn't have been going so fast. The poor cat. Now she must go and admit what she had done, confront an angry or distressed owner, an owner who presumably lived in the house behind that hedge.

She opened the gate and went up the path. It was a cottage but not a pretty one: red brick with a low slate roof, bay windows downstairs with a green front door between them. In each bay window sat a cat; one black, one orange and white like the cat that had run in front of her car. They stared at her, unblinking, inscrutable, as if they did not see her, as if she were not there. She could still see the black one when she was at the front door. When she put her finger to the bell and rang it, the cat did not move, nor even blink its eyes.

No one came to the door. She rang the bell again. It occurred to her that the owner might be in the back garden, and she walked round the side of the house. It was not really a garden but a wilderness of long grass and tall weeds and wild trees. There was no one. She looked through a window into a kitchen where a tortoiseshell cat sat on top of the fridge in the sphinx position, and on the floor, on a strip of matting, a brown tabby rolled sensuously, its striped paws stroking the air.

There were no cats outside as far as she could see, not living ones at least. In the left-hand corner, past a kind of lean-to coal-shed and a clump of bushes, three small wooden crosses were just visible among the long grass. Anna had no doubt they were cat graves.

She looked in her bag, and finding a hairdresser's

appointment card, wrote on the blank back of it her name, her parents' address, and their phone number, added, "Your cat ran out in front of my car. I'm sorry, I'm sure death was instantaneous." Back at the front door, the black cat and the orange-and-white cat still staring out, she put the card through the letter-box.

It was then that she looked in the window where the black cat was sitting. Inside was a small over-furnished living-room that looked as if it smelt. Two cats lay on the hearthrug, two more were curled up together in an armchair. At either end of the mantel-piece sat a china cat, white and red with gilt whiskers. Anna thought there ought to have been another one between them, in the centre of the shelf, because this was the only clear space in the room, every other corner and surface being crowded with objects, many of which had some association with the feline: cat ashtrays, cat vases, photographs of cats in silver frames, postcards of cats, mugs with cat faces on them, and ceramic, brass, silver, and glass kittens. Above the fireplace was a portrait of a marmalade-and-white cat done in oils, and on the wall to the left hung a cat calendar.

Anna had an uneasy feeling that the cat in the portrait was the one that lay dead in the road. At any rate, it was very like it. She could not leave the dead cat where it was. In the boot of her car were two plastic carrier-bags, some sheets of newspapers, and a blanket she sometimes used for padding things she did not want to strike against each other while she was driving. As wrapping for the cat's body the plastic bags would look callous, the newspapers worse. She would sacrifice the blanket. It was a clean dark blue blanket, single size, quite decent and decorous.

The cat's body wrapped in this blanket, she carried it up the path. The black cat had moved from the left-hand bay and taken up a similar position in one of the upstairs windows. Anna took another look into the living-room. A second examination of the portrait confirmed her guess that its subject was the one she was carrying. She backed away. The black cat stared down at her, turned its head, and yawned hugely. Of course it did not know she carried one of its companions, dead and now cold, wrapped in an old car blanket, having met a violent death. She had an uncomfortable feeling, a ridiculous feeling, that it would have behaved in precisely the same way if it had known.

She laid the cat's body on the roof of the coal-shed. As she came back round the house, she saw a woman in the garden next door. This was a neat and tidy garden, with flowers and a lawn. The woman was in her fifties, white-haired, slim, wearing a twin set.

"One of the cats ran out in front of my car," Anna said. "I'm afraid it's dead."

"Oh, dear."

"I've put the . . . body . . . the body on the coal-shed. Do you know when they'll be back?"

"It's just her," the woman said. "It's just her on her own."

"Oh, well. I've written a note for her. With my name and address."

The woman was giving her an odd look. "You're very honest. Most would have just driven on. You don't have to report running over a cat, you know. It's not the same as a dog."

"I couldn't have just gone on."

"If I were you, I'd tear that note up. You can leave it to me, I'll tell her I saw you."

"I've already put it through the door," said Anna.

She said goodbye to the woman and got back into her car. She was on her way to her parents' house, where she would be staying for the next two weeks. Anna had a flat on the other side of the town, but she had promised to look after her parents' house while they were away on holiday, and—it now seemed a curious irony—her parents' cat.

If her journey had gone according to plan, if she had not been delayed for half an hour by the accident and the cat's death, she would have been in time to see her mother and father before they left for the airport. But when she got there, they had gone. On the hall-table was a note for her in her mother's hand to say that they had had to leave; the cat had been fed and there was a cold roast chicken in the fridge for Anna's supper. The cat would probably like some too, to comfort it for missing them.

Anna did not think her mother's cat, a huge fluffy creature of a ghostly whitish-grey tabbyness, named Griselda, was capable of missing anyone. She could not believe it had affections. It seemed to her without personality or charm, to lack endearing ways. To her knowledge, it had never uttered beyond giving an occasional thin squeak that signified hunger. It had never been known to rub its body against human legs, or even against the legs of the furniture. Anna knew that it was absurd to call an animal selfish, an animal naturally put its survival first, self-preservation being its prime instinct, yet she thought of Griselda as deeply, intensely, callously selfish. When it was not eating it slept, and it slept in those most comfortable places where the people that owned it would have liked to sit but from which they could not bring themselves to dislodge it: At night it lay on their bed and if they moved, dug its long sharp claws through the bed-clothes into their legs.

Anna's mother did not like hearing Griselda referred to as "it." She corrected Anna and stroked Griselda's head. Griselda, who purred a lot when recently fed and ensconced among cushions, always stopped purring at the touch of a human hand. This would have amused Anna if she had not seen that her mother seemed hurt by it, withdrew her hand and gave an unhappy little laugh.

When she had unpacked the case she brought with her, had prepared and eaten her meal and given Griselda a chicken leg, she began to wonder if the owner of the cat she had run over would phone. The owner might feel, as people bereaved in great or small ways sometimes did feel, that nothing could bring back the dead. Discussion was useless, and so, certainly, was recrimination. It had not, in fact, been her fault. She had been driving fast, but not *illegally* fast, and even if she had been driving at thirty miles an hour, she doubted if she could have avoided the cat, which had streaked so swiftly out of the hedge.

It would be better to stop thinking about it. A night's sleep, a day at work, and the memory of it would recede. She had done all she could. She was very glad she had not just driven on, as the next-door neighbour had seemed to advocate. It had been some consolation to know that the woman had many cats, not just the one, so that perhaps losing one would be less of a blow.

When she had washed the dishes and phoned her friend Kate, wondered if Richard, the man who had taken her out three times and to whom she had given this number, would phone and had decided he would not, she sat down beside Griselda, not *with* Griselda but on the same sofa as she was on, and watched television. It got to ten and she thought it unlikely the cat woman—she had begun thinking of her as that—would phone now.

There was a phone extension in her parents' room but not in the spare room where she would be sleeping. It was nearly eleven-thirty and she was getting into bed when the phone rang. The chance of its being Richard, who was capable of phoning late, especially if he thought she was alone, made her go into her parents' bedroom and answer it.

A voice that sounded strange, thin and cracked, said what sounded like "Maria Yackle."

"Yes?" Anna said.

"This is Maria Yackle. It was my cat that you killed."

Anna swallowed. "Yes. I'm glad you found my note. I'm very sorry, I'm very sorry. It was an accident. The cat ran out in front of my car."

"You were going too fast."

It was a blunt statement, harshly made. Anna could not refute it. She said, "I'm very sorry about your cat."

"They don't go out much, they're happier indoors. It was a chance in a million. I should like to see you. I think you should make amends. It wouldn't be right for you just to get away with it."

Anna was very taken aback. Up till then the woman's remarks had seemed reasonable. She did not know what to say.

"I think you should compensate me, don't you? I loved her, I love all my cats. I expect you thought that because I had so many cats it wouldn't hurt me so much to lose one."

That was so near what Anna had thought that she felt a kind of shock, as if this Maria Yackle or whatever she was called had read her mind. "I've told you I'm sorry. I am sorry, I was very upset, I *hated* it happening. I don't know what more I can say."

"We must meet."

"What would be the use of that?" Anna knew she sounded rude, but she was shaken by the woman's tone, her blunt, direct sentences.

There was a break in the voice, something very like a sob. "It would be of use to me."

The phone went down. Anna could hardly believe it. She had heard it go down but still she said several times over, "Hallo? Hallo?" and "Are you still there?"

She went downstairs and found the telephone directory for the area and looked up "Yackle." It wasn't there. She sat down and worked her way through all the *Y*'s. There were not many pages of *Y*'s, apart from "Youngs," but there was no one with a name beginning with *Y* at that address on the rustic road among the cottages.

She could not get to sleep. She expected the phone to ring again, Maria Yackle to ring back. After a while she put the bed-lamp on and lay there in the light. It must have been three, and still she had not slept, when Griselda came in, got on the bed, and stretched her length along Anna's legs. She put out the light, deciding not to answer the phone if it did ring, to relax, forget the run-over cat, concentrate on nice things. As she turned face-downwards and stretched her body straight, she felt Griselda's claws prickle her calves. As she shrank away from contact, curled up her legs and left Griselda a good half of the bed, a thick rough purring began.

The first thing she thought of when she woke up was how upset that poor cat woman had been. She expected her to phone back at breakfast time, but nothing happened. Anna fed Griselda, left her to her house, her cat-flap, her garden and wider territory, and drove to work. Richard phoned as soon as she got in. Could they meet the following evening? She agreed, obscurely wishing he had said that night, suggesting that evening herself only to be told he had to work late, had a dinner with a client.

She had been home for ten minutes when a car drew up outside. It was an old car, at least ten years old, and not only dented and scratched but with some of the worst scars painted or sprayed over in a different shade of red. Anna, who saw it arrive from a front window, watched the woman get out of it and approach the house. She was old, or at least elderly—is elderly older than old or old older than elderly?—but dressed like a teenager. Anna got a closer look at her clothes, her hair, and her face when she opened the front door.

It was a wrinkled face, the colour and texture of a chicken's wattles. Small blue eyes were buried somewhere in the strawberry redness. The bright white hair next to it was as much of a contrast as snow against scarlet cloth. She wore tight jeans with socks pulled up over the bottoms of them, dirty white running shoes, and a big loose sweat-shirt with a cat's face on it, a painted smiling bewhiskered mask, orange and white and green-eyed.

Anna had read somewhere the comment made by a young girl on an older woman's boast that she could wear a miniskirt because she had good legs: "It's not your legs, it's your face." She thought of this as she looked at Maria Yackle, but that was the last time for a long while she thought of anything like that.

"I've come early because we shall have a lot to talk about," Maria Yackle said and walked in. She did this in such a way as to compel Anna to open the door further and stand aside. "This is *your* house?"

She might have meant because Anna was so young, or perhaps there was some more offensive reason for asking.

"My parents'. I'm just staying here."

"Is it this room?" She was already on the threshold of Anna's mother's living-room.

Anna nodded. She had been taken aback, but only for a moment. It was best to get this over. But she did not care to be dictated to.

"You could have let me know. I might not have been here."

There was no reply because Maria Yackle had seen Griselda.

The cat had been sitting on the back of a wing-chair, between the wings, an apparently uncomfortable place though a favourite, but at sight of the newcomer had stretched, got down, and was walking towards her. Maria Yackle put out her hand. It was a horrible hand, large and red, with rope-like blue veins standing out above the bones, the palm calloused, the nails black and broken and the sides of the forefingers and thumbs ingrained with brownish dirt. Griselda approached and put her smoky-whitish muzzle and pink nose into this hand.

"I shouldn't," Anna said rather sharply, for Maria

Yackle was bending over to pick the cat up. "She isn't very nice. She doesn't like people."

"She'll like me."

And the amazing thing was that Griselda did. Maria Yackle sat down and Griselda sat on her lap. Griselda the unfriendly, the cold-hearted, the cat who purred when alone and who ceased to purr when touched, the ice-eyed, the stand-offish walker-by-herself settled down on this unknown, untried lap, having first climbed up Maria Yackle's chest and onto her shoulders and rubbed her ears and plump furry cheeks against the sweat-shirt with the painted cat face.

"You seem surprised."

Anna said, "You could say that."

"There's no mystery. The explanation's simple." It was a shrill, harsh voice, cracked by the onset of old age, articulate, the usage grammatical, but the accent raw cockney. "You, and your mum and dad too, no doubt, you all think you smell very nice and pretty. You have your bath every morning with bath essence and scented soap. You put talcum powder on and spray stuff in your armpits, you rub cream on your bodies and squirt on perfume. Maybe you've washed your hair too, with shampoo and conditioner and—what-do-they-call-it?—mousse. You clean your teeth and wash your mouth, put a drop more perfume behind your ears, paint your faces—well, I dare say your dad doesn't paint his face, but he shaves, doesn't he? More mousse and then aftershave.

"You put on your clothes. All of them clean, spotless. They've either just come back from the dry-cleaner's or else out of the washing-machine, with biological soap and spring-fresh fabric-softener. Oh, I know—I may not do it myself, but I see it on the TV.

"It all smells very fine to you, but it doesn't to her. Oh, no. To her it's just chemicals, like gas might be to you, or paraffin. A nasty strong chemical smell that puts her right off and makes her shrink up in her furry skin. What's her name?"

This question was uttered on a sharp bark. "Griselda," said Anna, and, "How did you know it's a she?"

"Face, look," said Maria Yackle. "See her little nose. See her smily mouth and her little nose and her fat cheeks? Tom-cat's got a big nose, got a long muzzle. Never mind if he's been neutered, still got a big nose."

"What did you come here to say to me?" said Anna.

Griselda had curled up on the cat woman's lap, burying her head, slightly upward turned, in the crease between stomach and thigh. "I don't go in for all that stuff, you see." The big red hand stroked Griselda's head, the stripy bit between her ears. "Cat likes the smell of me because I haven't got my clothes in soapy water every day. I have a bath once a week, always have and always shall, and I don't waste my money on odorizers and deodorizers. I wash my hands when I get up in the morning, and that's enough for me."

At the mention of the weekly bath, Anna had reacted instinctively and edged her chair a little farther away. Maria Yackle saw, Anna was sure she saw, but her response to this recoil was to begin on what she had in fact come about: her compensation.

"The cat you killed, she was five years old and the queen of the cats, her name was Melusina. I always have a queen. The one before was Juliana, and she lived to be twelve. I wept, I mourned her, but life has to go on. The queen is dead, I said, long live the queen! I never promote one, I always get a new kitten. Some cats are queens, you see, and some are not. Melusina was eight weeks old when I got her from the Animal Rescue people, and I gave them a donation of twenty pounds. The vet charged me twenty-seven pounds fifty for her injections; all my cats are immunized against feline enteritis and lepto-spirosis, so that makes forty-seven pounds fifty. And she had her booster at age two, which was another twenty-seven fifty—I can show you the receipted bills, I always keep everything—and that makes seventy-five pounds. Then there was my petrol getting her to the vet; we'll say a straight five pounds though it was more; and then we come to the crunch, her food. She was a good little trencher-woman."

Anna would have been inclined to laugh at this ridiculous word but she saw to her horror that the tears were running down Maria Yackle's cheeks. They were running unchecked out of her eyes, over the rough red wrinkled skin, and one dripped unheeded onto Griselda's silvery fur.

"Take no notice. I do cry whenever I have to talk about her. I loved that cat. She was the queen of the cats. She had her own place, her throne; she used to sit in the middle of the mantelpiece with her two china ladies-in-waiting on each side of her. You'll see one day, when you come to my house.

"But we were talking about her food. She ate a large can a day, it was too much, more than she should have had, but she loved her food, she was a good little eater. Well, cat food's gone up over the years, of course—what hasn't?—and I'm paying fifty pee a can now, but I reckon it'd be fair to average it out at forty pee. She was eight weeks old when I got her, so we can't say five times three hundred and sixty-five. We'll say five times three fifty-five, and that's doing you a favour. I've already worked it out at home, I'm not that much of a wizard at mental arithmetic. Five three hundred and fifty-fives are one thousand, seven hundred and seventy-five, which multiplied by forty makes seventy-one thousand pee, or seven hundred and ten pounds. Add to that the seventy-five plus the vet's bill of fourteen pounds when she had a tapeworm, and we get a final figure of seven hundred and ninety-nine pounds."

Anna stared at her. "You're asking me to give you nearly eight hundred pounds."

"That's right. Of course we'll write it down and do it properly."

"Because your cat ran under the wheels of my car?"

"You murdered her," said Maria Yackle.

"That's absurd. Of course I didn't murder her." On shaky ground, she said, "You can't murder an animal."

"You did. You said you were going too fast."

Had she? She had been, but had she said so?

Maria Yackle got up, still holding Griselda, cuddling Griselda, who nestled purring in her arms. Anna watched with distaste. You thought of cats as fastidious creatures but they were not. Only something insensitive and undiscerning would put its face against that face, nuzzle those rough, grimy hands. The black fingernails brought to mind a phrase, now unpleasantly appropriate, her grandmother had used to children with dirty hands: in mourning for the cat.

"I don't expect you to give me a cheque now. Is that what you thought I meant? I don't suppose you have that amount in your current account. I'll come back tomorrow or the next day."

"I am not going to give you eight hundred pounds," said Anna.

She might as well not have spoken.

"I won't come back tomorrow, I'll come back on Wednesday." Griselda was tenderly placed on the seat of an armchair. The tears had dried on Maria Yackle's face, leaving salt trails. She took herself out into the hall and to the front door. "You'll have thought about it by then. Anyway, I hope you'll come to the funeral. I hope there won't be any hard feelings."

That was when Anna decided Maria Yackle was mad. In one way this was disquieting, in another a comfort. It meant she was not serious about the compensation, the eight hundred pounds. Sane people do not invite you to their cat's funeral. Mad people do not sue you for compensation.

"No, I shouldn't think she'd do that," said Richard when they were having dinner together. He was not a lawyer but had studied law. "You didn't admit you were exceeding the speed limit, did you?"

"I don't remember."

"At any rate you didn't admit it in front of witnesses. You say she didn't threaten you?"

"Oh, no. She wasn't unpleasant. She cried, poor thing."

"Well, let's forget her, shall we, and have a nice time?"

Although no note awaited her on the doorstep, no letter came and there were no phone calls, Anna knew the cat woman would come back on the following evening. Richard had advised her to go to the police if any threats were made. There would be no need to tell them she had been driving very fast. Anna thought the whole idea of going to the police bizarre. She rang up her friend Kate and told her all about it and Kate agreed that telling the police would be going too far.

The battered red car arrived at seven. Maria Yackle was dressed as she had been for her previous visit, but because it was rather cold, wore a jacket made of synthetic fur as well. From its harsh, too-shiny texture there was no doubt it was synthetic but from a distance it looked like a black cat's pelt.

She had brought an album of photographs of her cats for Anna to see. Anna looked through it—what else could she do? Some were recognizably of those she had seen through the windows. Those that were not she supposed might be of animals now at rest under the wooden crosses in Maria Yackle's back garden. While she was looking at the pictures, Griselda came in and jumped onto the cat woman's lap.

"They're very nice, very interesting," Anna said. "I can see you're devoted to your cats."

"They're my life."

A little humouring might be in order. "When is the funeral to be?"

"I thought on Friday. Two o'clock on Friday. My sister will be there with her two. Cats don't usually take to car travel, that's why I don't often take any of mine with me, and shutting them up in cages goes against the grain, but my sister's two Burmese love the car, they'll go and sit in the car when it's parked. My friend from the Animal Rescue will come if she can get away, and I've asked our vet, but I don't hold out much hope there. He has his goat clinic on Fridays. I hope you'll come along."

"I'm afraid I'll be at work."

"It's no flowers by request. Donations to the Cats' Protection League instead. Any sum, no matter how small, gratefully received. Which brings me to money. You've got a cheque for me."

"No, I haven't, Mrs. Yackle."

"Miss. And its Yakob. *J-A-K-O-B*. You've got a cheque for me for eight hundred pounds."

"I am not giving you any money, Miss Jakob. I'm very, very sorry about your cat, about Melusina, I know how fond you were of her, but giving you compensation is out of the question. I'm sorry."

The tears had come once more into Maria Jakob's eyes, had spilled over. Her face contorted with misery. It was the mention of the wretched thing's name, Anna thought. That was the trigger that started the weeping. A tear splashed onto one of the coarse red hands. Griselda opened her eyes and licked up the tear.

Maria Jakob pushed her other hand across her eyes. She blinked. "We'll have to think of something else then," she said.

"I beg your pardon?" Anna wondered if she had really heard. Things couldn't be solved so simply.

"We shall have to think of something else. A way for you to make up to me for murder."

"Look, I will give a donation to the Cats' Protection League. I'm quite prepared to give them—say, twenty pounds." Richard would be furious but perhaps she would not tell Richard. "I'll give it to you, shall I, and then you can pass it on to them?"

"I certainly hope you will. Especially if you can't come to the funeral."

That was the end of it then. Anna felt a great sense of relief. It was only now that it was over that she realized quite how it had got to her. It had actually kept her from sleeping properly. She phoned Kate and told her about the funeral and the goat clinic and Kate laughed and said, "Poor old thing." Anna slept so well that night that she did not notice the arrival of Griselda who, when she woke, was asleep on the pillow next to her face but out of touching distance.

Richard phoned and she told him about it, omitting the part about her offer of a donation. He told her that being firm, sticking to one's guns in situations of this kind, always paid off. In the evening she wrote a cheque for twenty pounds, but instead of the Cats' Protection League, made it out to Maria Jakob. If the cat woman quietly held on to it, no harm would be done. Anna went down the road to post her letter, for she had written a letter to accompany the cheque, in which she reiterated her sorrow about the death of the cat and added that if there was anything she could do, Miss Jakob had only to let her know. Richard would have been furious.

Unlike the Jakob cats, Griselda spent a good deal of time out of doors. She was often out all evening and did not reappear until the small hours, so it was not until the next day, not until the next evening, that Anna began to be alarmed at her absence. As far as she knew, Griselda had never been away so long before. For herself she was unconcerned, she had never liked the cat, did not particularly like any cats, and found this one obnoxiously self-centred and cold. It was for her mother, who unaccountably loved the creature, that she was worried. She walked up and down the street, calling Griselda, though the cat had never been known to come when it was called.

It did not come now. Anna walked up and down the next street, calling, and around the block and farther afield. She half-expected to find Griselda's body, guessing that it might have met the same fate as Melusina. Hadn't she read somewhere that nearly forty thousand cats are killed on British roads annually? On Saturday morning she wrote one of those melancholy lost-cat notices and attached it to a lamp standard, wishing she had a photograph. But her mother had taken no photographs of Griselda.

Richard took her to a friend's party and afterwards, when they were driving home, he said, "You know what's happened, don't you? It's been killed by that old madwoman. An eye for an eye, a cat for a cat."

"Oh, no, she wouldn't do that. She loves cats."

"Murderers love people. They just don't love the people they murder."

"I'm sure you're wrong," said Anna, but she remembered how Maria Jakob had said that if the money was not forthcoming she must think of something else, a way to make up to her for Melusina's death, and she had not meant a donation to the Cats' Protection League.

"What shall I do?"

"I don't see that you can do anything. It's most unlikely you could prove it, she'll have seen to that. You can look at it this way: she's had her pound of flesh. . . ."

"Fifteen pounds of flesh," said Anna. Griselda had been a large, heavy cat.

"Okay, fifteen pounds. She's had that, she's had her revenge. It hasn't actually caused you any grief, you'll just have to make up some story for your mother."

Anna's mother was upset but nowhere near as upset as Maria Jakob had been over the death of Melusina. To avoid too much fuss, Anna had gone further than she intended, told her mother that she had seen Griselda's corpse and talked to the offending motorist, who had been very distressed. A month or so later Anna's mother got a kitten, a grey tabby tomkitten, who was very affectionate from the start, sat on her lap, purred loudly when stroked, and snuggled up in her arms, though Anna was sure her mother had not stopped having baths or using perfume. So much for the Jakob theories.

Nearly a year had gone by before she again drove down the road where Maria Jakob's house was. She had not intended to go that way. Directions had been given her to a smallholding where they sold early strawberries on a roadside stall but she must have missed her way, taken a wrong turning and come out here.

If Maria Jakob's car had been parked in the front she would not have stopped. There was no garage for it to be in, it was not outside; therefore the cat woman must be out. Anna thought of the funeral she had not been to, she had often thought about it, the strange people and strange cats who had attended it.

In each of the bay windows sat a cat, a tortoiseshell and a brown tabby. The black cat was eyeing her from upstairs. Anna did not go to the front door but round the back. There, among the long grass, as she had expected, were four graves instead of three, four wooden crosses, and on the fourth was printed in black gloss paint: *Melusina, the Queen of the Cats, murdered in her sixth year. RIP.*

That "murdered" did not please Anna. It brought back all the resentment at unjust accusations of eleven months before. She felt much older, she felt wiser. One thing was certain, ethics or no ethics: if she ever ran over a cat again, she'd drive on; the last thing she'd do was go and confess.

She came round the side of the house and looked in at the bay window. If the tortoiseshell had still been on the windowsill she probably would not have looked in, but the tortoiseshell had removed itself to the hearthrug.

A white cat and the marmalade-and-white lay curled up side by side in an armchair. The portrait of Melusina hung above the fireplace, and this year's cat calendar was up on the left-hand wall. Light gleamed on the china cats' gilt whiskers, and between them, in the empty space that was no longer vacant, sat Griselda.

Griselda was sitting in the queen's place in the middle of the mantelpiece. She sat in the sphinx position with her eyes closed. Anna tapped on the glass and Griselda opened her eyes, stared with cold indifference, and closed them again.

The queen is dead, long live the queen!

DYING
HAPPY

was sitting by his bedside. He had a pure white room all to himself.

"This place reminds me of something that happened to a friend of mine."

"What friend?" I said.

"You didn't know him. He's dead now anyway. Or dead to all intents and purposes." He gave me a sly sideways look. It was a look that dared me to ask what that last remark meant. I didn't ask and he said, "I'll tell you about him." He put his head back on the pillow and looked at the white, white ceiling. "A long time ago, twenty years at least, he had a relationship with this woman."

I had to interrupt. "Oh, come on," I said. "I have a relationship with you. Come to that, I have a relationship with the milkman."

"Well, an affair then. I hate the word too. I picked

it up from Miriam." Miriam was his wife. "An affair," he said. "A love passage. He was married, of course. But he was in love with this woman, about as much in love as anyone can be, I gather. Fathoms deep. He was a very romantic man. He didn't tell his wife, but of course she found out and put a stop to it."

"What was her name?" I said.

"The girl-friend? Susanna. Her name was Susanna. She wasn't any younger than his wife or better-looking or cleverer or anything. And none of them were young, you know. Even then, at the time, they weren't young. I said she put a stop to it but that was only for a while. They started up again in secret, and this time when the wife found out, Susanna herself stopped it. She said it wasn't fair to any of them and she didn't answer his phone calls or his letters or anything, and after a while it sort of petered out, as these things do. Anyway, this was all of twenty years ago, as I said.

"His wife would bring up Susanna's name every time they disagreed. You can imagine. And he wasn't above comparing his wife unfavourably with Susanna if she annoyed him. But after a time they stopped mentioning her, though my friend never stopped thinking about her. He said that never a day passed without him thinking of her. And she came into his dreams. He got to look forward to those dreams because he said at least that way he got to see her sometimes."

"The poor devil," I said.

"Yes, well, he was romantic."

It was nearly as white outside as in. There was snow on the ground and lumps of snow on the tree branches. He turned his face to the dazzling snow, screwing up his eyes. "He got some awful thing the matter with him. I'm speaking about the present day now, more or less. They gave him a limited time to live, a matter of months . . . you know how they won't commit themselves. He got it into his head he had to see Susanna before he died. He had to see her; he could die happy or at least contented if he could see her."

"Did he know where she was?" I said.

"Oh, yes, he knew. You have to understand that though they never spoke of her, he and his wife, he knew all about her, everything that had happened to her. He knew she had moved and that she had married. It was an agony to him when she married. He knew the day and the hour and he sat watching the clock. Her husband died and he tried not to rejoice. He sent anonymous flowers, not for her dead husband but to her. That was the only contact, if contact it can be called, between them in all those years. Now to see her again was an obsession with him. He dreamt of it, he thought of nothing else.

"His wife had said she'd do anything for him, anything he wanted she'd try to get him. 'Get me Susanna,' he said. 'I want to see Susanna before I die.' Well, that wasn't at all what she'd meant by anything he wanted. You can imagine. She shouted and wept and said if Susanna came there—he was at home then, he went into hospital later—if Susanna came, she'd kill her. 'Oh, grow up,' he said. 'The way you dramatize everything. We're all old now, we can't do anything. Look at me, be reasonable, why d'you grudge me a bit of happiness? I won't trouble you for long.'

"'You're my husband,' she said, 'you're mine. It's me you ought to want to see.' 'God knows I see you every minute of every day,' he said. 'I'll pull the phone wires out of the wall,' she said. 'If you write to her I won't post the letter, I'll burn any letter you write to her. And if you get her here, I'll kill her. I'll hit her over the head like I would a burglar if I caught him in my house.'"

He was staring hard at me now and breathing rather quickly. The white glare on his face made him look like death.

"Take it easy," I said.

"I will. I am." He managed a grin. "It wasn't only his wife he saw. The neighbours used to come in. And his friends from the old days. He got one of them to post the letter. And Susanna answered by return of post. There was no question of his wife keeping the letter from him; she couldn't tell who his letters were from. That letter made him so happy. He had waited twenty years for it, he felt he could have died he was so happy. And maybe it would have been for the best if he had. Maybe it would.

"He phoned her, he spoke to her, they fixed a time for Susanna to come. Hearing her voice was another kind of ecstasy. He told his wife when she was coming and said that the best thing would be for her to go out. 'I'll kill her before she walks through that door,' his wife said. I don't think I said they'd never met, did I, Susanna and his wife? Well, they never had, never even heard each other's voice on the phone. Of course he didn't believe his wife would kill her. I mean, would you? No one would. He didn't even believe she'd do Susanna an injury."

"What happened when Susanna came?" I said.

"The hospice was set in parkland. Cedar trees stood very black and ragged against the snow. You could see visitors' cars approach from the time they entered the distant gate. He was watching a car worm its way along the road between the snow-banks.

"He heard her come to the door and he waited. It was ages before she came up. And when she did his wife was with her. Susanna was changed, but he didn't mind about that, and they were all changed. How could it be otherwise? She didn't touch him, she didn't even touch his hand. She and his wife sat there talking across him. They talked about the books they read and knitting and painting in water-colours and golf—he'd never realized they had so much in common. They even looked alike. After a while they went downstairs. Susanna came again next day but she only looked in on him for two minutes. She and his wife had dinner together downstairs and watched the gardening programme on television. The day after that he had to go into hospital."

"This friend," I said, "it was you, wasn't it?"

"How did you know?"

"It always is," I said. "And I suppose I posted that letter for you."

He nodded, looking very tired now. The door opened and two women came in: big florid Miriam with a fur hat on her red hair and a fur coat that made her look like a marmalade cat and big zip-up boots, and another one like a tortoiseshell cat, as furry and booted but a fraction taller. Miriam introduced me.

"We mustn't stay long, darling. We're learning Italian and we've got our lesson at two. We're planning on Rome together for Easter, so there's no time to waste. Give him the chocolates, Susanna, and then we must rush. If the snow clears tomorrow, we'll be on the golf course all weekend, so I don't suppose we'll see you again till Monday."

THE
COPPER
PEACOCK

Peter Seeburg lived in a flat without a kitchen.

"Kitchens make you fat," he said.

Bernard asked if that was one of the principles of the Seeburg Diet, which Peter was going to the United States to promote. Peter smiled.

"All one needs," he said, "is an electric kettle in the bathroom and a fridge somewhere else." He added rather obscurely, "Eating out keeps you thin because it is so expensive."

He was lending the flat to Bernard while he was in America. They walked around it and Peter explained how things worked. The place was very clean. "A woman comes in three times a week. Her name's Judy. She won't get in your way."

"Do I have to have her?"

"Oh dear yes, you do. If I get rid of her for three

months I'll never get her back again, and I can't do with that."

He would have to put up with it, he supposed. Peter's kindness in lending him the flat, rent-free, to write his new biography in was something he still found overwhelming. It was quiet here—was this the only street in west London not being renovated, not a noisy jumble of scaffolding and skips? No sounds of music penetrated the ceilings. The other tenants in the block did not, apparently, spend their mornings doing homework for their carpentry courses. The windows gave onto plane trees and Regency façades.

"She's very efficient. She'll probably wash your clothes if you leave them lying about. But you won't be sleeping here, will you?"

"Absolutely not," said Bernard.

As it was he felt guilty about leaving Ann alone all day with the children. But it was useless to attempt working at home with a two-year-old and a three-year-old under the same roof with him. Memories were vivid of Jonathan climbing on his shoulders and Jeremy trying out felt-tipped pens on his notes while he was last correcting page proofs. Still, he would be back with them in the evenings. He would have to make up for everything to Ann in the evenings.

"There's no question of my sleeping here," he said to Peter as if he hadn't heard him the first time.

Peter gave him the keys. On Monday morning he was flying to Los Angeles, the first leg of his tour. Bernard arrived in a taxi two hours after he left, bringing with him two very large bags full of books. The biography he was embarking on was the life of a rather obscure Edwardian poet. His last book had been the life of a rather obscure Victorian diarist, and some

critic had said of it that the excellence of the writing
and the pace of the narrative transcended the fact that
few had heard of its subject. Bernard had a gift for
writing with elegance and panache about fairly undis-
tinguished literary figures and for writing books that
sold surprisingly well.

It was his habit to spread his works of reference
out on the floor. He would create little islands of books
and notebooks, a group here that dealt with his subject's childhood, a cluster there of criticism of his
works, an archipelago of the views of his peers. Two or
three rooms ideally should be reserved for this purpose. Some of the books lay open, others with slips of
paper inserted between their pages. The notes were in
piles that might seem haphazard to others but to
Bernard were arranged in a complex but precise
order.

As soon as he was inside Peter's flat and the front
door closed behind him, Bernard began spreading his
books out after this fashion. Already he felt a deep
contentment that one particular notebook, containing
new material he had assembled on his subject's ances-
try, would lie undisturbed surrounded by its minor
islets, instead of being seized upon by Jonathan, as had
happened to one of its predecessors, and given a new
function as a kneading board for play dough. Bernard
created a further island in the bedroom. He wouldn't
otherwise be using the bedroom and the books could
just lie there for weeks, gathering dust. This was
another image that afforded him an intense intellec-
tual pleasure. His typewriter set up on the dining-table
in the absence of a desk, he found himself making an
enthusiastic start, something by no means usual with
him.

On the following morning, though, he recalled that the books couldn't just lie there. No dust would gather because Judy would be coming in to see it did not. Resenting her presence in advance of her arrival, he picked up all the books, slipping in bits of paper at significant pages, and sealing the bedroom pile by laying on top of it, open and face-downwards, the earliest published biography of his poet. Beginning as he meant to go on, he was at the typewriter, busily working away, rather more busily and noisily in fact than the prose he was committing to paper warranted, when just after ten-thirty he heard the front door open and close.

Some few minutes had passed before she came into the dining-room. She knocked first. Bernard was surprised by her youth. She looked no more than twenty-seven. He had expected a stout aproned motherly creature in her fifties. What clichés we make of life! She was slim, pretty, dark-haired, wearing jeans and a blouse. But the prettiness was worn and the hair was rough and dry. She was too thin for the tight jeans to be tight on her, and her hip-bones stuck out like the sharp curved frame of a lyre.

"Could you do with a coffee?" she said. No introduction, no greeting. Her smile was friendly and cheerful. "I get Peter his coffee about now."

Bernard castigated himself for a snob. Why on earth should she call Peter "Mr. Seeburg" anyway? "Thank you. That's very kind of you." He put out his hand. "I'm Bernard Hope."

"Pleased to meet you, Bernard. Peter's told me all about you." For all the readily used Christian names, her manner was a little shy, her handshake tentative. "Do you mind if I come in here for the milk?" she said.

"I have to make the coffee in the bathroom, but he keeps his fridge in here."

"No, please, go ahead."

"Peter said you'd want all your books left just as they were but you're very tidy, aren't you?" She didn't wait for an answer but said confidingly, with a slight giggle, "I'll never get over him not having a kitchen. You have to laugh. I get a laugh out of it every time I come here."

All this seemed ominous to Bernard. Fearing a prolonged disturbance of his peace, he set himself to typing furiously when she returned with the coffee. Perhaps this was effective as a deterrent, or else she genuinely wanted to get on with her work, for she spoke no further word to him until the time came for her departure at half past twelve. Appearing at the dining-room door in a padded jacket, she mimed—to his astonishment—the action of pounding a keyboard.

"Keep on with the good work. See you Wednesday."

Bernard couldn't resist getting up to review the flat after she had gone. He was pleasantly surprised. Surfaces had been polished and there was a fresh flowery scent in the air. His books lay as he had left them, the slips of paper in place, the important notebook still face-downwards and guarding the stack beneath it. He re-created his islands. The coffee-cups had disappeared, been washed and restored to their home in a china cabinet. On one of the tables in the living room was a tray covered with a cloth and on the tray was a plate of the kind of sandwiches that are called "dainty," with a glass of orange juice, a polished red apple, and a piece of cheese.

His lunch. Bernard felt quite touched, although

he quickly realized that she must do this for Peter and no doubt regarded it as part of the duties for which she was paid. Since Jeremy was born, Ann had never got lunch for him, he had always got his own. Not that he expected his wife to wait on him, of course not, she had the children and the house, more than enough to do. Two of the sandwiches were smoked salmon and two egg and cress. Judy must have brought their ingredients with her and assembled them in the bathroom. Next day he was preparing to say something gracious but he took a look at her and there was only one thing anyone could say.

"What have you done to yourself?"

She put her hand up to her face. She had a black eye. The cheek-bone was dark red and shiny with bruising, and the corner of her lip was cut. Her finger touched the bruise. "Fell against the door, didn't I?" she said. It was a curious usage of language, that interrogatory. He wasn't sure if he had ever heard it before. "Kitchen door with a handle sticking out." She giggled. "That's what comes of having kitchens. Maybe Peter's got the right idea."

He asked her if she had seen a doctor. And when she said she hadn't, she hadn't the patience to sit waiting about for an hour or more just to get a prescription she'd have to pay for anyway, he thanked her for getting his lunch. "You're welcome, love," she said, and "It's all in the day's work." He watched her test the tenderness of her cut lip with a questing tongue. "Ready for your coffee, are you, or d'you want to wait a bit?"

He had it later in the living-room, perusing his notebook, while she cleaned the dining-room. Things were just as he had left them when he went back except that she had closed the work of reference he had left open by the typewriter and had marked his place with a sheet torn from a scribbling block. Lunch that day was pâté sandwiches, and there was a pear on the tray and a piece of walnut cake. Next time he got gruyère cheese, mandarin yoghurt, and a bunch of red grapes. It was something of a chore going out to buy pizza on the intervening days. The awful things that had happened to Judy's face made him think she might be accident-prone and at first he waited to hear her drop things, but she moved almost soundlessly about the flat, putting her head round the door to tell him when she was going to use the vacuum cleaner, apologizing in advance, and in the event getting it over as fast as possible. She made less noise about the place than Ann did, Ann who was exasperated by sweeping and dusting and who loudly cursed both tools and furniture. As soon as this thought came to him he felt guilty, so that night he took home a bottle of champagne and a begonia in a pot.

Peter phoned one afternoon during Bernard's third week there. It was early morning in Denver, Colorado, where he had arrived to spread the gospel of the Seeburg Diet. He wanted a book sent out to him. It was a book on calories and food combining that Bernard would find on one of the shelves in the bedroom up on the right-hand side.

"Everything okay?" he said. "How's the poet? How are you getting on with Judy?"

Bernard said the biography was progressing quite satisfactorily, thank you very much. Judy was fine, marvellous, very efficient. There seemed no point in adding that this morning, though her face had healed and the discoloration around her eye faded, he had noticed bruises on her left arm and a strip of plaster on her left hand. That was hardly the kind of thing to talk about with Peter.

"She's what my poet's contemporaries would have called a treasure." His poet had in fact been attracted by servants, had a long-standing clandestine affair with his sister's nursery maid.

"Mind you say hello to her from me next time she comes."

Her hand was still plastered and her face looked as if bruised anew. Only it couldn't be, he must be imagining this, or she was tired or one of those people whose skin marks at a touch. It couldn't really be that the damaged eye had been injured again.

"Peter said to say hello."

The handy Americanism was evidently new to her but she worked it out.

"Sent his love, did he? You pass mine on next time he gives you a phone. I've got caviar for your sandwiches today, that lumpfish, really, but I reckon it tastes the same." She showed him the jar. "Lovely colour, isn't it? More like strawberry jam."

"You're good to me, Judy," he said.

"Get off. Good to you! You appreciate it, that's what I like, not like Peter, cottage cheese and beansprouts day after day for him. Still, what can you expect if you don't have a kitchen?"

He re-made his book islands once the front door had closed after her. The fate of his books, or rather the precariousness of the position of his bookmarks, no longer worried him. They were safe with Judy. Even if he failed to stack them before she came, they remained inviolate. And a strange thing had happened. He no longer wanted total silence and unobtrusiveness from her. He had arranged with her to bring his coffee at eleven, when he would break off for ten or even fifteen minutes for a chat. Mostly he talked to her and she listened while he spoke about his biography and his aims and his past career, necessarily simplifying things for this untutored audience. A look of wonder, or simple lack of comprehension, came into her thin hungry face. She admired him, he was sure of it, and he was curiously touched by her admiration. He told himself it made him feel humble.

And he had hardly realized before how much he liked gracious living. The turmoil of home, the chaos he had accepted as an inevitable corollary of modern life. Peter's flat was as he remembered his mother's home—clean, orderly, the woodwork shining, the upholstery not stained with spilt milk and chocolate smears. In the bathroom it was not necessary to pick one's way between the hazards of potty, disposable napkin packets, drying dungarees, and a menagerie of plastic amphibians in order to reach the lavatory. It was peaceful and silent, and it smelt, not of urine, milk, and disinfectant, but of floor wax and the civilized dry bitter-sweetness of the chrysanthemums Judy had bought at the same time as the caviar.

"You're quite in love with her," said Ann.

"Get off," said Bernard before he realized whom he was quoting. "I only said she was a good housewife." She would hardly understand if he said he looked forward to ten-thirty, then to coffee time, to his conversation with this naïve listener. It was more than he could understand himself, how an interruption had become a pleasure.

Peter phoned from Chicago. It was just before seven in the morning there, so not yet one in London, and Judy was still in the flat. Bernard thought Peter must be phoning so early to wish him a happy birthday, and he felt quite touched. Ann hadn't exactly forgotten what this day was, she had only forgotten to get him a present. But the reason for Peter's call was to say the food-combining book had arrived and would Bernard send him the file of homeopathic pills from the bathroom cabinet.

"I'm halfway through my life today," said Bernard.

"Many happy returns. If I'd known I'd have sent you a card. Say hello to Judy for me."

"You don't look forty," she said to him, standing in the doorway in her padded jacket.

For a moment he didn't know what she meant. When he did, he was mildly affronted, then amused. "Thirty-five," he said. "Halfway through man's allotted span. You think I'll make it to eighty, do you?"

"I didn't ought to have listened," she said. "Sorry. It was a bit of a cheek."

He had a curious impulse to put his arm round her thin shoulders and press her quickly close to him. But of course he couldn't do that. "Get off," he said. "Why shouldn't you listen? It wasn't private."

She said goodbye and left and he put his books back on the floor. Rather reluctantly he returned to work. His subject had been acquainted with the great literary figures of his day and Bernard was about to write of his first meeting, while at university in Dublin, with James Joyce. Joyce, he reflected, had lived with and later married a servant—a chambermaid, wasn't she? It had been a happy partnership between the giant of letters and his Nora, the nearly illiterate woman.

Ham sandwiches and thinly sliced avocado, sesame-seed biscuits, a glass of apple juice. For once he wasn't hungry for it. What he would have liked—he suddenly saw the rightness of it—was to have taken Judy out for lunch. Why hadn't he thought of it while she was still there? Why hadn't he thought of it as a way of celebrating his birthday? Although she had been gone twenty minutes he went to the window and looked out to see if, by remote chance, she might still be waiting at the bus stop. There was no one in the bus shelter but an old man reading the timetable.

They could have gone to the Italian restaurant round the corner. She was so thin, he wondered if she ever got a decent meal. He would have enjoyed choosing the dishes for her and selecting the wine. A light sparkling Lambrusco would have been just the thing to please her, and he would have put up with it even though it might be rather showy and obvious for him. But she had gone and it was too late. In her absence he felt restless, unable to concentrate. He had no phone number for her, no address; he didn't even know her surname. If she didn't come on Tuesday, if she never came again, he wouldn't know how to find her, he would have lost her forever.

This anxiety was absurd, for of course she did come. His weekend had been unpleasant, with Jonathan developing a viral infection and Ann announcing that she meant to go back to work in the spring. He had to stay at home on Monday to look after the sick child while Ann took the other for a dental appointment. The quietness and order of Peter's flat received him, seemed to welcome him with a beckoning and a smile. Only another month and Peter would be home, but he didn't want to think of that.

At ten-thirty Judy let herself in. She was always punctual. The bruises faded, the scars healed, she looked very pretty. He thought what an exceedingly good-looking woman she was with that flush on her cheeks and her eyes bright. Instead of going to his work-table and his typewriter, he had waited for her in the living-room, and when she came in he did something he normally did for women but had never done for her. He laid his book aside and stood up. It seemed almost to alarm her.

"Are you okay, Bernard?"

He smiled, nodded. He had never actually witnessed her arrival before and now he watched her remove her jacket, take indoor shoes out of her bag and put them on, remarking as she did so, reverting to the aspect of the place that endlessly amused her, that if Peter had a kitchen she would have been able to change there. The scuffed boots she wore outdoors tucked inside the bag, she took from it a small package, a box, it looked like, wrapped in silver-spotted pink paper. Her manner becoming awkward, she said to Bernard, thrusting the package into his hands.

"Here, this is for you. Happy birthday."

She was blushing. She had gone a fiery red. Bernard untied the ribbon and took off the paper. Inside the box, on a piece of cotton wool, lay a metal object about six inches long and an inch wide. Its shaft was flat like the blade of a knife, and attached to a hook on the top that curved backwards in a U-shape was a facsimile of a peacock with tail spread fan-wise, the whole executed in beaten copper and a mosaic of blue, green, and purple glass chips. To Bernard it looked at first like some piece of cheap jewellery, a woman's hair ornament or clip. He registered its tawdry ugliness, felt at a loss for words. What was it? He looked up at her.

"It's a bookmark, isn't it?" She spoke with intense earnestness. "You put it in your book to show where you've got to."

He was still mystified.

"Look, I'll show you." She picked up the book he had been reading, a memoir of the Stephen family who had also been acquainted with his poet. At the place he had reached, she inserted the copper knife blade and, closing the book on it, hooked the peacock over the top of the spine. "See how it works?"

"Yes, thanks. Thank you very much."

Confidingly, she said, "I couldn't help seeing, while I've been working about, the way you'd always leave one of your books open and face-down. Well, you don't like to turn down the corner of the page, do you, not when it's a library book? It doesn't seem right. So I thought, it's his birthday, I know what I'll do, I'll get him one of these. I'd seen them in this shop, hadn't I? One of those'd be just the thing for him and his books, I thought."

It was a curious kind of shock. The thing was hideous. It seemed more of an affront because it was books it must inevitably be associated with, books that he had such a special dedicated feeling about. If it didn't sound too silly and pretentious, he could almost have said books were sacred. The peacock's tail, curved breast, and stupid face glittered against the dull brown of the binding. The manufacturer had even managed to get red into it. The bird's eyes were twin points of ruby red. Bernard took the book and his new bookmark into the dining-room. He found himself closing the door for the first time in weeks. Of course he would have to use the bloody thing. She would look for it, expect to see it every time she came. If he left one of his books face-downwards she would want to know why he wasn't using his new bookmark.

"You do like it, don't you, Bernard?" she said when she brought his coffee.

"Of course I like it." What else could he say?

"I thought you'd like it. When I saw it I thought that's just the thing for Bernard."

Why did they always have to say everything twice, these people? She had seated herself as usual opposite him to wait for him to begin their conversation. But this morning he didn't want to talk, he had nothing to say. It even seemed to him that she had somehow betrayed him. She had shown him how little his words meant to her, if in spite of everything he had said and shown himself to be, she could still have bought him this tasteless, vulgar object. He knew he was being ridiculous but he couldn't help feeling it. He took the coffee from her, feigning an absent manner, and returned to his typewriter.

Honest with himself—he tried to be that—he admitted what had been in his mind. He had meant to make love to her. To what end? Was she to have been his Nora? He had never progressed so far, even in his thoughts. Simply he had thought of love and pleasure, of taking her about and giving her a good time. Was he mad? They were poles apart, a great gulf fixed between them, as she had proved by her gross misunderstanding of everything he was and stood for. Serve him right for having such aims and intents. It must be his subject who was taking him over, his poet who at sixteen had boasted to Frank Harris of getting his mother's kitchen-maid pregnant.

He nodded absently to her when, ready to leave, she put her head round the door. Peter phoned from Philadelphia not long after she had gone, and after he had talked to him Bernard felt better about things. He was able to make quite an amusing story out of the presenting of the peacock bookmark. And Peter commiserated with him, agreeing that there was no doubt about it, he would have to use the thing, and prominently, for the duration of his stay. Naturally, Bernard said nothing about his now vanished desire for Judy, any more than he did when he repeated the tale to Ann that night. Ann had the advantage over Peter in that she could actually be shown the object.

"It's copper," she said, "and it doesn't look mass-produced. It was probably quite expensive. You can't actually use it, it's dreadful."

"I don't want to hurt her feelings."

"What about your feelings? Aren't they important? If you don't want to say straight out you can't bear the thing, tell her you've left it at home or you've lost it. Let me have it and I'll lose it for you."

Next day he followed her advice and left the bookmark at home. Judy didn't say anything about it, though it was her day for dusting the bedroom and he had left his notebook in the bedroom, lying face-downwards on the stack of other books. She watered Peter's plants and cleaned the windows. He didn't take a break from work when she brought his coffee, only looked up and thanked her. But he could see she had her eye on the books that covered half the dining-table. He was sure she was looking for the peacock. He repeated his thanks in as dismissive a tone as he could manage and she turned at once and left the room. The sandwiches she left him for lunch were tinned salmon and cucumber with a strawberry yoghurt and a chocolate bar. Bernard fancied the standard was less high than it had been.

It was a relief to be without her, as he always was on Thursdays. On Friday her face was once more the way it had been that first week, one eye black and swollen, her cheek bruised, her mouth cut. But he said nothing about it. He could see her gazing at all the books on the table, and after she had left the room he went quietly to the door and through the crack watched her slowly move the stacked volumes to dust the surface of a cabinet. By now it must have registered with her that he disliked the bookmark and had no intention of using it.

It was, of course, a mistake to be too friendly with these people, to put them on a level with oneself. He wasn't used to servants and that was the trouble. Who was, these days? Returning to work, he felt a flash of envy for his poet who, though comparatively poor, had nevertheless kept a man and two maids to look after him.

She spoke to him, as in the old days, when she brought his coffee. Tentatively, as if she thought him in a bad mood and she was placating him, she said, "I've been in the wars a bit."

He glanced up, took in once again that awful damaged eye. How could he once have thought her pretty? The notion came to him that she was trying to tell him something, appeal to him. Was she perhaps going to ask yet again if he liked the bookmark? He put up his eyebrows, made a rueful face. "Close the door after you, will you, Judy?"

Still, he had been wrong about the standard of lunch, having no fault to find with pastrami sandwiches, watercress salad, and a slice of pineapple. Ann's advice was sound. By not yielding he had shown the woman that imposing her atrocious taste on him wasn't on. But he hadn't bargained for what happened on Tuesday. She didn't come.

For a little while, when eleven was past and he was sure she wasn't coming, he felt awe at himself, at the stand he had taken. He had been strong and he had driven her away. Then he was pleased, he was relieved. Wasn't it absurd, a woman coming in three times a week to clean up after someone who didn't even sleep there, who scarcely ate there? Of course she would probably come back when Peter returned in three weeks' time. It was he she was ostracizing. She had taken offence because he wouldn't give in to her and use her hideous gift.

He had worked himself up a bit over her defection by the time he got home. "She could at least have phoned and made some excuse."

"They don't," said Ann. "Those people don't."

Any qualms he might have had about Judy's turning up later were soon allayed. It was clear she wasn't coming back. Bernard got into the way of buying himself something for his lunch on his way to the flat. He went without coffee. It wasn't as if he was used to it, as if Ann had ever made it for him. He left his books lying about all over the floors, face-downwards or with pieces of paper inserted between the pages. Of course he hadn't finished the life of his poet by the time Peter was due back, he wasn't even a quarter of his way through, but he had made such a good start he felt he could continue at home in spite of Jonathan and Jeremy, in spite of chaos and noise. He had broken the back of it.

Peter phoned the morning before he was due to leave New York. They talked about the weather, the heavy snowstorms that had been sweeping the east coast of America. Then Peter said, "That was terrible about Judy."

A strong word to use, but Peter was inclined to be intense.

"How did you know?" Bernard said.

"I saw it in the paper, of course. I do make a point of seeing English newspapers while I'm here."

They were at cross-purposes. "What did you see in the paper?"

Peter sounded astonished. "That he killed her, of course. I shouldn't have been surprised, I used to tell her he'd do it one day. I told her to leave him but she wouldn't. She must have talked to you about him, surely? I can't believe she came in all that time without a mark on her from what he was doing to her. They've charged him with murdering her. Don't you read your newspaper?"

He hadn't known her name, he said, he hadn't known where she lived or anything about her.

"What did you talk about? Didn't you ask?"

Bernard said goodbye and slowly let the receiver slide into its rest. What had they talked about, he and Judy? His work, English literature, books, his past career. He had talked and she had listened. Raptly, he thought now, her battered face lifted, her damaged eyes watching him. Why hadn't she said what happened to her at home? Why, instead of giving him that ridiculous tasteless thing, hadn't she thrown herself on his mercy, confided in him, offered herself to him?

He didn't say a word about it to Ann. "What happened to the peacock bookmark?"

"The children were playing with it and Jeremy kept putting it in his mouth, so I threw it out."

He wanted to hit her, he wanted to strike her in the face, and he clasped his hands together to keep himself from that.

WEEDS ✓

I am not at all sure," said Jeremy Flintwine, "that I would know a weed from whatever the opposite of a weed is."

The girl looked at him warily. "A plant."

"But surely weeds *are* plants."

Emily Hithe was not prepared to enter into an argument. "Let me try and explain the game to you again," she said. "You have to see if you can find a weed. In the herbaceous borders, in the rose-beds, anywhere. If you find one, all you have to do is show it to my father and he will give you a pound for it. Do you understand now?"

"I thought this was in aid of cancer research. There's not much money to be made that way."

She smiled rather unpleasantly. "You won't find any weeds."

It cost two pounds each to visit the garden. Jeremy, a publisher who lived in Islington, had been brought by the Wragleys, with whom he was staying. They had walked here from their house in the village, a very long walk for a Sunday afternoon in summer after a heavy lunch. Nothing had been said about fund-raising or playing games. Jeremy was already wondering how he was going to get back. He very much hoped to catch the twelve-minutes-past-seven train from Diss to London.

The Wragleys and their daughter Penelope, aged eight, had disappeared down one of the paths that led through a shrubbery. People stood about on the lawn drinking tea and eating digestive biscuits that they had had to pay for. Jeremy always found country life amazing. The way everyone knew everyone else, for instance. The extreme eccentricity of almost everybody, so that you suspected people, wrongly, of putting it on. The clothes. Garments he had supposed obsolete—cotton frocks and sports jackets—were everywhere in evidence. He had thought himself suitably dressed, but now he wondered. Jeans were not apparently correct wear except on the under-twelves and he was wearing jeans, an old, very clean, pair, selected after long deliberation, with an open-necked shirt and an elegantly shabby Italian silk cardigan. He was also wearing, in the top buttonhole of the cardigan, a scarlet poppy tugged up by its roots from the grass verge by Penelope Wragley.

The gift of this flower had been occasioned by one of George Wragley's literary anecdotes. George, who wrote biographies of poets, was not one of Jeremy's authors, but his wife Louise, who produced best-sellers for children and adored her husband, was. Therefore Jeremy found it expedient to listen more or less politely to George's going on and on about Francis Thompson and the Meynells. It was during the two-mile-long trudge to the Hithes' garden that George related how one of the Meynell children, with appropriate symbolism, had presented the opium-addicted Thompson with a poppy in a Suffolk field, bidding him, "Keep this forever!" Penelope had promptly given Jeremy his buttonhole, which her parents thought a very sweet gesture, though he was neither a poet nor an opium addict.

They had arrived at the gates and paid their entry fee. A lot of people were on the terrace and the lawns. The neatness of the gardens was almost oppressive, some of the flowers looking as if they had been washed and ironed and others as if made of wax. The grass was the green of a billiard table and nearly as smooth. Jeremy asked an elderly woman, one of the tea-drinkers, if Rodney Hithe did it all himself.

"He has a man, of course," she said.

The coolness of her tone was not encouraging, but Jeremy tried. "It must be a lot of work."

"Oh, old Rod's got that under control," said the girl with her, a granddaughter perhaps. "He knows how to crack the whip."

This Jeremy found easy to believe. Rodney Hithe was a loud man. His voice was loud and he wore a jacket of loud blue-and-red-checked tweed. Though seeming affable enough, calling the women "darling" and the men "old boy," Jeremy suspected he was the kind of person it would be troublesome to get on the wrong side of. His raucous voice could be heard from end to end of the garden, and his braying, unamused laugh.

"I wouldn't want to find a weed," said the granddaughter, voicing Jeremy's own feelings. "Not for a pound. Not at the risk of confronting Rod with it."

Following the path the Wragleys had taken earlier, Jeremy saw people on their hands and knees, here lifting a blossoming frond, there an umbelliferous stalk, in the forlorn hope of finding treasure underneath. The Wragleys were nowhere to be seen. In a far corner of the garden, where geometric rose-beds were bounded on two sides by flint walls, stood a stone seat. Jeremy thought he would sit down on this seat and have a cigarette. Surely no one could object to his smoking in this remote and secluded spot. There was in any case no one to see him.

He was taking his lighter from his jeans pocket when he heard a sound from the other side of the wall. He listened. It came again, an indrawing of breath and a heavy sigh. Jeremy wondered afterwards why he had not immediately understood what kind of activity would prompt the utterance of these sighs and half-sobs, why he had at first supposed it was pain and not pleasure that gave rise to them. In any case, he was rather an inquisitive man. Not hesitating for long, he hoisted himself up so that he could look over the wall. His experience of the countryside had not prepared him for this. Behind the wall was a smallish enclosed area or farmyard, bounded by buildings of the sty and byre type. Within an aperture in one of these buildings, on a heap of hay, a naked girl could be seen lying in the arms of a man who was not himself naked but dressed in a shirt and a pair of running shoes.

"Lying in the arms of" did not accurately express what the girl was doing, but it was a euphemism Jeremy much preferred to "sleeping with" or anything franker. He dropped down off the wall but not before he had noticed that the man was very deeply tanned and had a black beard and that the girl's resemblance to Emily Hithe made it likely this was her sister.

This was no place for a quiet smoke. He walked back through the shrubbery, lighting a cigarette as he went. Weed-hunting was still in progress under the bushes and among the Alpines in the rock garden, this latter necessarily being carried out with extreme care, using the fingertips to avoid bruising a petal. He noticed none of the women wore high heels. Rodney Hithe was telling a woman who had brought a Pekingese that the dog must be carried. The Wragleys were on the lawn with a middle-aged couple who both wore straw hats, and George Wragley was telling them an anecdote about an old lady who had sat next to P. G. Wodehouse at a dinner party and enthused about his work throughout the meal under the impression he was Edgar Wallace. There was some polite laughter. Jeremy asked Louise what time she thought of leaving.

"Don't you worry, we shan't be late. We'll get you to the station all right. There's always the last train, you know, the eight forty-four." She went on confidingly, "I wouldn't want to upset poor old Rod by leaving the minute we arrive. Just between you and me, his marriage hasn't been all it should be of late, and I'd hate to add to his troubles."

This sample of Louise's arrogance rather took Jeremy's breath away. No doubt the woman meant that the presence of anyone as famous as herself in his garden conferred an honour on Rodney Hithe that was ample compensation for his disintegrating home life. He was reflecting on vanity and authors and self-delusion when the subject of Louise's remark came up to them and told Jeremy to put his cigarette out. He spoke in the tone of a prison officer addressing a habitual offender in the area of violent crime. Jeremy, who was not without spirit, decided not to let Hithe cow him.

"It's harmless enough out here, surely."

"I'd rather you smoked your filthy fags in my wife's drawing-room than in my garden."

Grinding it into the lawn would be an obvious solecism. "Here," Jeremy said, "you can put it out yourself," and he did his best to meet Hithe's eyes with an equally steady stare. Louise gave a nervous giggle. Holding the cigarette end at arm's length, Hithe went off to find some more suitable extinguishing ground, disappeared in the direction of the house and came back with a gun.

Jeremy was terribly shocked. He was horrified. He retreated a step or two. Although he quickly understood that Hithe had not returned to wreak vengeance but only to show off his new twelve-bore to the man in the straw hat, he still felt shaken. The ceremony of breaking the gun, he thought it was called, was gone through. The straw-hatted man squinted down the barrel. Jeremy tried to remember if he had ever actually seen a real gun before. This was an aspect of country life he found he disliked rather more than all the other things. Tea was still being served from a trestle-table outside the French windows. He bought himself a cup of tea and several of the more nourishing biscuits. It seemed unlikely that any train passing through north Suffolk on a Sunday evening would have a restaurant or even a buffet car. The time was coming up to six. It was at this point that he noticed the girl he had last seen lying in the arms of the bearded man. She was no longer naked but wearing a T-shirt and a pair of shorts. In spite of these clothes, or perhaps because of them, she looked rather older than when he had previously seen her. Jeremy heard her say to the woman holding the dog, "He ought to be called a Beijingese, you know," and give a peal of laughter.

He asked the dog's owner, a woman with a practical air, how far it was to Diss.

"Not far," she said. "Two or three miles. Would you say two miles, Deborah, or nearer three?"

Deborah Hithe's opinion on this distance Jeremy was never to learn, for as she opened her mouth to speak, a bellow from Rodney silenced all conversation.

"You didn't find that in this garden!"

He stood in the middle of the lawn, the gun no longer in his hands but passed on for the scrutiny of a girl in riding breeches. Facing him was the young man with the tan and the beard, whom Jeremy knew beyond a doubt to be Deborah's lover. He held up, in teasing fashion for the provocation of Hithe, a small plant with a red flower. For a moment the only sound was Louise's giggle, a noise that prior to this weekend he would never have suspected her of so frequently making. A crowd had assembled quite suddenly, surely the whole population of the village, it seemed to Jeremy, which Louise had told him was something over three hundred.

The man with the beard said, "Certainly I did. You want me to show you where?"

"He should never have pulled it out, of course," Emily whispered. "I'm afraid we forgot to put that in the rules, that you're not supposed to pull them out."

"He's your sister's boy-friend, isn't he?" Jeremy hazarded.

The look he received was one of indignant rage. "My *sister*? I haven't got a sister."

Deborah was watching the pair on the lawn. He saw a single tremor shake her. The man who had found the weed made a beckoning gesture to Hithe to follow him along the shrubbery path. George Wragley lifted his shoulders in an exaggerated shrug and began telling the girl in riding breeches a long pointless story about Virginia Woolf. Suddenly Jeremy noticed it had got much colder. It had been a cool, pale-grey, still day, a usual English summer day, and now it was growing chilly. He did not know what made him remember the gun, notice its absence.

Penelope Wragley, having ingratiated herself with the woman dispensing tea, was eating up the last of the biscuits. She seemed the best person to ask who Deborah was, the least likely to take immediate inexplicable offence, though he had noticed her looking at him and particularly at his cardigan in a very affronted way. He decided to risk it.

Still staring, she said as if he ought to know, "Deborah is Mrs. Hithe, of course."

The implications of this would have been enough to occupy Jeremy's thoughts for the duration of his stay in the garden and beyond, if there had not come at this moment a loud report. It was, in his ears, a shattering explosion, and it came from the far side of the shrubbery. People began running in the direction of the noise before its reverberations had died away. The lawn emptied. Jeremy was aware that he had begun to shake. He said to the child, who took no notice, "Don't go!" and then set off himself in pursuit of her.

The man with the beard lay on his back in the rose

garden and there was blood on the grass. Deborah
knelt beside him, making a loud keening wailing noise,
and Hithe stood between two of the geometric rose-
beds, holding the gun in his hands. The gun was not
exactly smoking but there was a strong smell of gun-
powder. A tremendous hubbub arose from the party
of weed-hunters, the whole scene observed with a kind
of gloating horrified fascination by Penelope Wragley,
who had reverted to infantilism and watched with her
thumb in her mouth. The weed was nowhere to be
seen.

Someone said superfluously, or perhaps not superfluously, "Of course it was a particularly tragic kind
of accident."

"In the circumstances."

The whisper might have come from Louise. Jeremy decided not to stay to confirm this. There was
nothing he could do. All he wanted was to get out of
this dreadful place as quickly as possible and make his
way to Diss and catch a train, any train, possibly the last
train. The Wragleys could send his things on.

He retreated the way he had come, surprised to
find himself tiptoeing, which was surely unnecessary.
Emily went past him, running towards the house and
the phone. The Pekingese or Beijingese dog had set up
a wild yapping. Jeremy walked quietly around the
house, past the drawing-room windows, through the
open gates and into the lane.

The sound of that shot still rang horribly in his
ears, the sight of red blood on green grass was still
before his eyes. The unaccustomed walk might be
therapeutic. It was a comfort, since a thin rain had
begun to fall, to come upon a signpost that told him he
was going in the right direction for Diss and it was only

a mile and a half away. There was no doubt the country seemed to show people as well as nature in the raw. What a nightmare that whole afternoon had been, culminating in outrageous violence! How horrible, after all, the Wragleys and Penelope were, and in a way he had never before suspected! Why were one's authors so awful? Why did they have such appalling spouses and ill-behaved children? Penelope had stared at him when he asked her about Deborah Hithe as disgustedly as if, like that poor man, he had been covered in blood.

And then Jeremy put his hand to his cardigan and felt the front of it, patted it with both hands like a man feeling for his wallet, looked down, saw that the scarlet poppy she had given him was gone. Her indignation was explained. The poppy must have fallen out when he hoisted himself up and looked over the wall.

It was a moment or two before he understood the cause of his sudden fearful dismay.

THE
FISH-SITTER

Next door to the Empress Court Disco Roller Rink in Seoul Road, Southend, was the south-east Essex branch of Daleth Foods and next to that the Aquarium. It was a parade of interesting and even exotic emporiums, as are often found in the hinterland of seaside resorts. Goods were sold, services offered, and entertainment provided.

For instance, in a flatlet above Magda's Sports Equipment, Ruta Yglesias the clairvoyante told fortunes; next door was a beauty clinic entirely devoted to eyes, the painting of their lids and lashes and the enhancement of their sparkle; and at the photographer's, last in the parade, little girls might dress up in tutus with ribbon laces cross-gartered to their knees, and dream as they posed that they were Veronica Spencer dancing *Giselle*.

The Aquarium's real name was Malvina's Marine

Museum, a grand title for what was quite a modest affair. On a sunny afternoon, when the beaches and the shops were crowded, the amusement arcades busy and the streets empty, Mrs. Trevor was showing her fish-sitter round the tank room. It was lit, even on a day like this, for each tank had its own strip light as well as its own aeration pump. These were necessarily at floor level, set to illuminate the green, ever-moving, ever-bubbling water below, and sending up into the tank room a glaucous, rather misty, glow. In the room below, visitors to the aquarium could be seen only occasionally and then dimly through glass and water as they moved, mostly in silence, between the Sarcopterygii, the Selachii, and the Decapoda. Some paused to read the printed and illustrated labels attached to the wall by each tank. Others pressed their faces against the cool glass and the marine creatures swam close to inspect them.

"Do you know, Cyril, this will be the first holiday I've had since I started this place," Mrs. Trevor was saying. "Well, come to that, the first since I stopped working for you-know-who."

Cyril knew very well who and was no more anxious to speak the name of the famous romantic novelist than was her erstwhile home help. This attitude, on both their parts, brought him a pang of guilt, for would he have ever known Mrs. Trevor but for Louise Mitchell? This job, this temporary roof over his head, would certainly not have come about without her. Gazing down at the decapod among the weeds and branched coral below, he subtly changed the subject.

"I wonder that you chose to go on a Caribbean cruise, though. Won't it be rather a case of coals to Newcastle?"

"What very unfortunate and hackneyed metaphors you do pick on, Cyril," said Mrs. Trevor sharply. "You always have. What do you know about cruises, anyway?"

A meek man, or one who had that reputation, Cyril only smiled. He could have said something about the days of his employment on a cruise ship but he did not, though as he watched the crab's sideways progress among darting jewel-bright chimera he remembered the flying fish that had pursued the ship, and his friend who supervised the ladies' cloakroom next door with her collection of newts she called salamanders. He also recalled the food on the *Calypso Queen*, the leavings of which had come his way and hers.

"The green-carapaced crab," he said dreamily, "whose meat is sweet to eat."

"None of that, please. Part of my pleasure in running this place is in knowing these innocent creatures are safe from the fisherman's net and the treacherous lobster pot. You don't eat fish, do you, Cyril?"

"Not this sort, at any rate," said Cyril, his eyes now on some variety of many-tentacled octopus or squid. "Why does nothing live in the biggest tank?"

"I'm hoping to acquire a shark," said Mrs. Trevor. "Possibly even *Carcharhinus milberti*. Now you know what you have to do, don't you, Cyril? You close at five and then you come up here and feed the innocent creatures. Specific feeding instructions are all in the book. You turn off the lights but *not* the aeration and in certain cases cover the tanks with their lids. Is that understood?"

Cyril said it was and what about cleaning out the tanks? Some, he had noticed, were much overgrown with green algae, which had even covered the back of the stone crab.

"Carlos will come in and do that. It's a specialist job. You're the kind of person who would use Persil Automatic."

He knew she was angry with him for what he had said about crabmeat and not for the first time castigated himself for his tactless ways. They went downstairs and Mrs. Trevor resumed her seat behind the ticket window so that Shana from the rink could get back to her duties. Cyril, in the cosy sitting-room at the rear of the Aquarium, found his instruction book *The Care of Cold-Blooded Aquatic Vertebrae and Crustaceae* on a shelf between *Story and Structure* and Louise's novel *Open Windows*. But he did not read it, he looked unseeing at the pages.

As usual in one of his reveries, he trudged across familiar ground. Biggs was not such a bad name. It was an improvement on Smalls, for instance, with its connotations of underclothes. Several saints had been called Cyril. He had looked them up in encyclopaedias. There were Saint Cyril of Jerusalem and Saint Cyril of Alexandria, both Doctors of the Church. There was that Saint Cyril who was responsible for Christianizing the Danubian Slavs, and who invented the Cyrillic writing system. It is not everyone who can boast of sharing his name with an alphabet.

Was it his name that had doomed him to obscurity, and worse, to mockery? People laughed when they heard he was an insurance-claims inspector, as if someone called that could hardly be anything else. But his venture at changing his name and adopting another profession had met with disaster. "Maxwell Lawrie" sounded distinguished. For a time his books featuring Vladimir Klein, international espionage agent, had brought him success and promised fame. *Glasnost* had put an end to all hope there, for who cares for spies when there may soon be nothing and no one left to spy on?

You cannot get back into insurance when you have been absent from it for so long, but Cyril had not even tried. Before he came back to Southend and Malvina's Marine Museum, he had been living on alms given him by the Espionage Authors' Benevolent Association in a hotel room in Madagascar Road, NW2, paid for by Brent Council. There he had often sat and wondered what might be the destiny of one called Cyril Biggs. Surely there must be more than to be the prototype of the dull little man in the novel, the one with thinning hair and the ugly wife, the one with shoes always dull with the dust of mean streets. He sensed sometimes that he had never had his full potential realized, though he did not know what that potential might be.

Malvina Trevor left for Southampton as soon as the Aquarium closed. She had dressed herself in a grey-green suit with a frilly blouse. Once her taxi had disappeared round the corner of Seoul Road, Cyril went up to the tank room and carefully scattered fish food into the tanks. He switched off the lights, but not the aeration and heating plant, and where instructed closed the lids. It was a complex routine which, once learned, became simple. Day after day it was repeated. From ten till five Cyril sat at the ticket window. At five-thirty he fed the fish and closed up the tank room. On two days a week Shana came in to relieve him, and several times Ruta Yglesias asked him in to supper.

Louise Mitchell was there on one occasion, for the sisters had always been close, and their mother with them. On another Ruta had invited some people called Ann and Roger, whose surname Cyril no more learned than he did the Christian name of another guest, Mrs. Greenaway. But it was quite a party and, to his surprise, Cyril enjoyed himself. He was not really gloomy by nature, only shy and lacking confidence. Before Malvina returned—and she would be back in less than a week—Cyril made up his mind to return Ruta's hospitality.

Giving dinner parties was not something he was accustomed to. For days he agonized over what he should give Ruta, Mrs. Church, and Mavis Ormitage to eat. With Shana ensconced behind the ticket window, he roved the front at Southend, eyeing the fish stalls, and in equal doubt and confusion paced between the freezers in the Presto Supermarket. Food was expensive, or that kind was. The price of crabs and lobsters horrified him. He informed the stone crab in the Aquarium of the amount asked for its fellows when "dressed" and offered for sale on the stalls. The crab's reply was to scamper sideways across its weedy coralline floor. I wonder if it is really green-carapaced, thought Cyril, or if its back is the reddy-pink colour of those I saw this afternoon. It is hard to tell because of the algae that covers it.

The main course was to be pasta, the kind the Italians call *alle vongole* because it has small scallops mixed up in it. Cyril bought the pasta at Daleth Foods, but naturally the Orthodox Jews who ran it would have nothing to do with shellfish. The seafood came from his favourite stall on the front—it was the cheapest—where he also bought a large dressed crab. Cyril mixed its sweet meat with Hellmann's mayonnaise to make it go further and everyone pronounced it delicious. But when Mavis made a remark about its being rather strange to eat shellfish with "all that lot swimming about in there," he felt uncomfortable. Had he been wrong to choose this menu? Had he made himself look a fool?

"Does that mean zoo-keepers must be vegetarians then, Mavis?" asked Mrs. Church.

Mavis giggled. "You know what I mean. If you had supper with a zoo-keeper you wouldn't imagine you were eating lion chops, but here—well, you know what I mean."

They all did and Cyril could not help noticing that Ruta left a great many of her *vongole* on the side of her plate. What had induced him to make a lime mousse in a fish shape for pudding? It must have been seeing the copper mould in the window of the shop at the end of the parade where Mr. Cybele sold antique scoops. Mr. Cybele had lent him the fish mould and the pale-green shape looked pretty. Unfortunately no one wanted to eat it after what Mavis Ormitage had said.

Cyril felt that his party had been a failure. That, of course, was nothing new. Most of his ventures, large and small, were failures. The arrival in the morning of Carlos with his tank-cleaning equipment distracted his mind from unhappy reminiscing. Cyril hung a notice on the Aquarium door, announcing that it would be closed till after lunch. He inspected the tanks before re-opening. The improvement in their appearance was quite wonderful. Everything sparkled, fresh and gleaming. Every aquatic vertebra looked rejuvenated—except the stone crab, whose carapace was still overgrown with dense green fur.

Its appearance troubled him. When he went about his feeding routine he put one finger into the water, touched the shell and found he could easily scrape some of the crust of algae off with his fingernail. Carlos had cleaned the biggest tank in the middle of the room as well, and Cyril, closing the lid on the crab, wondered when the new shark would arrive. Before Malvina's return or after? She was coming back in two days' time. Ruta and Mrs. Church were driving to Southampton in Mrs. Church's new Audi to fetch her.

Cyril slept badly that night. He saw himself as a social misfit. He wondered about his future, which seemed to have no existence beyond Malvina's return. A great crowd came to the Aquarium in the morning, and entrance had to be restricted. Visitors had heard about the cleaning operation, and for the first time Cyril saw a queue at the front door. When the last visitor had left at five, he paced up and down the sitting-room, uncertain what to do, torn by conflicting demands. Then, impulsively, he rushed upstairs. He lifted the large, algae-coated decapod out of its tank, took it to the bathroom, and washed it under the running tap. It was the work of a moment. The crab's carapace was indeed green, a pure soft emerald green with a curious design like an ideograph in a dark purplish shade on its back.

Tenderly, Cyril restored it to its home. The crab scuttled through its woodland of weed across its coral floor, attended by a little shoal of fish coloured like jewels. If Malvina inquired, he decided, he would tell her it had somehow happened during Carlos's operations. But surely she would be delighted? Cyril suddenly found himself hyperanxious to please Malvina, to confront her with perfection, to have attained, so to speak, supererogatory heights of achievement. Merely to have done the appointed job was not enough. He spent most of Saturday night sweeping and vacuum-cleaning aquarium, tank room, and the rest of the house, and on Sunday morning wrote in his best lettering a label for the biggest tank: "*Carcharhinus milberti*, the Sandbar Shark," which he followed by a careful description of its habitat and habits.

Mrs. Trevor came back at seven in the evening, dressed exactly as she had been when she left. She entered the Aquarium alone and trembling with anger. Cyril had expected Ruta and Mrs. Church to be with her, but evidently they had thought it wisest to make themselves scarce. Malvina gave each tank a rapid penetrating glance, the stone crab a longer look. She went upstairs and Cyril followed. So far she had not uttered a word and Cyril had received no reply to his inquiries as to her health and enjoyment of her trip. In the tank room she stood looking down at the stone crab, turned to face Cyril and said in shrill tones,

"How dare you?"

Putting the blame on Carlos forgotten, Cyril stammered that the crab was not harmed, indeed seemed happier for the cleansing operation.

"Don't give me that. Don't even think of trying it. I know what you have done. Ruta and her mother told me all about the seafood extravaganza you served up to them—and the ingredients used. This particular decapod, I have no doubt, was purchased or stolen from the tank of one of the fish restaurants on the front. Monterroso's, most probably."

"It isn't true, Malvina. They're lying. I wouldn't do that."

"I'm not a fool, you know. It isn't even the same variety. Look at the colour! You're too ignorant to know that there are no less than four thousand, five hundred species of crab, aren't you? You thought, when you slaughtered that innocent creature to make mayonnaise, that one crab was very like another. Well, I shall expose you. I shall publish the whole story in the *Southend Times*. Needless to say, I shan't pay you. I shall not take you on as my permanent assistant, as was in my mind."

Cyril did not think. He did not hesitate. He gave her a shove and she fell into the biggest tank with a scream and a loud splash. If he saw her floundering there, he might soften, he thought, for he had never been hard-hearted, so he put the lid on, went down-stairs and out to the beach. In all his life he had never felt so happy, so free and so fulfilled. As he walked along the mud-flats with the sea breezes in his hair, he understood his destiny and the meaning of his name.

He was not a novelist's character, no figment of fiction, but one to inspire literature in his own right. One day books would be written about him, his past, his history, his obscurity, his striving for an identity, and his name: Cyril Biggs, the Marine Museum Mur-derer. Newspapers would give him headlines and television a favoured position in the six-o'clock news. At Madame Tussaud's, in the Chamber of Horrors, he would be placed by a water tank while a plastic facsimile of his victim floated within. He had found his vocation.

That night Cyril slept better than he had done for years. It was Shana's day to sit at the receipt of custom. Such news travels fast and, looking out of an upstairs window, Cyril was not surprised to see a queue wind-ing its way from the front door the length of the parade. Presently he crept down to the tank room.

He did not lift the lid from the biggest tank but

edged discreetly along the wall and peered into the stone crab's home, peered through sparkling, ever-bubbling jade-coloured water and gleaming spotless glass to the crowds beneath. There, pressed closely around the biggest tank, were Louise Mitchell, Ruta Yglesias, Fenella, Mrs. Church and Mrs. Greenaway, Henry Bennett with the Ruler and his painted queen, the three Jewish grocers, Veronica Spencer and her husband Tim, Margaret Cavendish, Jane, several Italian boys in T-shirts, and a host of others not recognizable to Cyril. Some were reading the label he had made for the sandbar shark but those who could get close had their faces pressed against the glass, contemplating what was within.

They were polite middle-class people, and as each had seen her or his fill, there was a stepping back and a parting to allow those behind to look. In one of these reshuffles, the tank was briefly revealed to Cyril's view and he saw floating inside it, flippers gently pulsating with the movement of the water, a vast grey-green shape with a frill about its neck like the ruff of a salamander.

AN UNWANTED WOMAN

I t's not a matter for the police."

He had said it before, to his wife, if not to this woman. The affair of Sophie Grant, bizarre, nearly incomprehensible, was outside the range of his experience. Deeply conservative, convinced of the superiority of past ways to those of the present, he was inclined to blame events on the decadence of the times he lived in. He repeated what he had said, added, "There's nothing we can do."

Jenny's friend, who was not crying yet, who seemed on the verge of crying or even screaming, a desperate woman, said in the voice she could only just control, "Then who am I to turn to? What can I do?"

"I've already suggested the Social Services," said Jenny, "but it's true what Hilary says: all they can do is take her into care, apply for a care order."

"She's not in need of care," Hilary said with bitterness, with venom. "She doesn't need protecting. It's me, I'm the one who's suffering. I ought to be taken into care and looked after." She had her voice and herself under control again. Her wineglass was empty. She took hold of it and, after a small hesitation, held it up. "I'm sorry, Jenny. I *need* it. It's not as if it was the hard stuff."

Jenny refilled the glass with Frascati. Hilary had got through half the bottle. They were sitting in the living-room of the Burdens' house in Glenwood Road, Kingsmarkham. It was just after nine on a winter's evening, Christmas not far off, as evinced by the first few cards, greetings from the superpunctual, on the mantelpiece. A wooden engine, gaily painted, a worn rabbit, and a Russian doll, its interlocking pieces separated, lay on the carpet, and these several objects Jenny now began picking up and dropping into a toy chest. Hilary watched her with increasing misery.

"I know I'm a nuisance. I know I'm disturbing you when you'd like a quiet evening on your own. I'm sorry, but you—well, Jenny—you're all I've got. I don't know who else to talk to. Except to Martin, and he . . . sometimes I think he's *glad*. Well, he's not, I shouldn't say that, but when she was there she was so hateful to him, it must be a relief. You see"—she looked away from them—"I'm so *ashamed*. That's why I can't tell other people, because of being ashamed."

Burden thought he would have a drink, if only to make Hilary feel better. He fetched himself a beer from the fridge. When he came back, Jenny had her arm round Hilary and Hilary had tears on her face.

"What is there to be ashamed of?"

"A woman whose child doesn't want to live with

her? What sort of a mother can she be? What sort of a home has she got? Of course I'm ashamed. People look at me and they think, what was going on in that house? They must have been abusing her, they must have ill-treated her."

"People don't *know,* Hilary. Hardly anyone actually knows. You're imagining all this."

"I can see it in their eyes."

Buoyed up by his drink, resigned to the ruin of his evening, Burden thought he might as well go the whole hog. Get it first-hand, though he could do nothing. Nothing could come of it but the slight relief of Hilary Stacey of relating it once again.

Jenny said suddenly, "Does her father know?"

"Her father wouldn't care. It's once in a blue moon he writes to her, she hasn't heard from him for months."

"Tell me exactly what happened, would you, Hilary? Jenny's told me, but I'd like you to." He was painfully aware of sounding like a policeman. On the other hand, she had *wanted* a policeman. "Tell me from the beginning."

"I thought you were going to say, '. . . in your own words,' Mike."

He inclined his head a little, not smiling.

"Sorry. Being so miserable makes me bitchy. What is this, therapy?"

"It might be that as well," said Burden. He was foraging in his knowledge of the law, thinking of such vague and insubstantial offences as enticement and corruption of a minor. "Let me have the facts. I'm not saying we can do anything, I'm sure we can't, but just tell me what happened, will you?"

She looked him in the eye. Her own eyes were a

startling turquoise-blue, large and prominent. It was easy to see why she never wore make-up, she was colourful enough without it—that white and rosy skin, those eyes, flaxen hair straight and shining. A woman with those attributes should have been good-looking, but Hilary missed beauty by the length of her face, which gave her a horsey look. She was very thin, thinner since this trouble started.

"It really began long before I married Martin," she said, "perhaps even when Peter and I were divorced five years ago. I didn't *want* a divorce, you know, I wanted to stay married for life. I know it sounds self-pitying but it was not my fault, it really wasn't, I was hard done by. Peter's girl-friend was pregnant. I still didn't want a divorce, but how long can you keep on fighting? I knew he'd never come back.

"Sophie was nine. She made a big thing about saying she hated Peter. She told people he'd left 'us,' not that he'd left me. She knew about the girl-friend Monica and she used to say her father preferred Monica to us. Well, she wouldn't see Peter for months, but gradually she came round. It was the baby, I think. He was her half-brother and she liked the idea of a brother. She started to enjoy spending weekends with Peter and Monica and the baby. I will say for Monica that she was very nice to her and of course it wasn't the usual situation where a child is jealous of a new sibling.

"I honestly think none of this would have happened if Peter and Monica were still here. I'm sure it's much more due to their going to America than to me marrying Martin. Peter had this job and no doubt it was the only course for him to take. He was always more or less indifferent to Sophie anyway, Monica was much nicer to her than her father was, and I don't think it bothered him that he wouldn't see his daughter for years. He could have afforded to pay her air fare to Washington, but he wouldn't.

"It was a blow to her. It was a second blow. Okay, I suppose you'll say my remarrying was the third. But what's a woman to do, Mike? I was on my own with Sophie, I had a full-time job, and the school holidays were a nightmare. So I got a part-time job, and even that was too much for me. And then, when things were about as grim as they'd ever been, I fell in love with Martin and he fell in love with me. I mean, it was like a dream, it was like something that you daren't dream about because it just won't happen; things as good as that don't happen. But it did. A nice kind clever successful good-looking man was in love with me and wanted to marry me and liked my daughter and thought she could be his daughter, and everything was wonderful.

"And she thought so too, Sophie thought so. She was happy, she was excited. I think she saw Martin as a wonderful new friend, hers as much as mine. Of course we were very careful in front of her, she was thirteen and that's a very difficult age. For ages I never let Martin even kiss me in her presence, and then when he did he'd always kiss her too.

"We got married and she was at the wedding and she loved every minute of it. Next day she started to hate him. She loathed him. She did everything to try to split us up, she told lies to us about the other one: she'd seen Martin out with a woman, she'd heard me call a man 'darling' on the phone, she'd heard me telling Jenny I married him for his money. Yes, *truly*. You wouldn't credit it, would you?

"When she saw she couldn't separate us, she did

what she's done—walked out and went to live with Ann Waterton. That's where she is and where she intends to stay, she says.

"I've pleaded with her, I've begged her, I've even tried to bribe her to come back. I've pleaded with Ann Waterton, I've been there, I've even set it all down in writing, in letters to her. To do Ann justice, she hasn't enticed her or anything like that; she's lonely, she likes Sophie's company, but she's told her she ought to go home. Anyway, she says she has. Sophie won't. She's got a key to Ann's house, she comes and goes as she pleases, and she's very good to Ann, she looks after her. She likes cooking, which Ann doesn't, and she cooks special meals for them. She takes Ann her breakfast in bed before she goes to school.

"I've asked Ann to change the locks on the door but she won't, she says Sophie would stay out in the street all night, and I think she's right, Sophie would do that. She'd wrap herself in blankets and sit on the garden wall or sleep in Ann's garage."

Burden said, "Have you asked her what it is she wants?"

"Oh, yes." Hilary Stacey gave a short, bitter laugh. "I've asked her. 'Get rid of Martin,' she says, 'and then I'll come home.'"

"What's the bugger done to her?" said Chief Inspector Wexford.

It was the following day, and he and Burden were on their way to London. Donaldson was driving and Wexford and Burden sat in the back of the car. Their mission was to interview two men suspected of being concerned in a break-in at Barclay's Bank in Kingsmarkham High Street a week before. One lived in

Hackney, the other was usually to be found around midday at a pub in Hanwell. Burden had been relating the story of Sophie Grant.

"Nothing," he said. "I'm sure of it. Oh, I know you can't tell. It's no good saying, 'I know the guy, I've had a meal in his house, I know he's not like that.' The most unexpected men are like that. But I'd say he just didn't have time. He didn't have the time or the opportunity. He and Hilary Grant, as she was, were newly married, sharing a bedroom—that was partly the trouble. Sophie stayed around for three weeks and then she left."

"But you say she seemed to like the chap before he married her mum?"

"I suppose she just didn't know, she didn't realize. She was nearly fourteen, but she didn't realize her mother would be sharing a bed with Martin Stacey. And I expect there was some kissing and cuddling and touching in her presence—well, there was bound to be."

"She thought it was a marriage for companionship, is that what you're saying? Yes, I can imagine. The mother was very careful, no doubt, *before* she was married; no physical contact when the girl was there, definitely no bed-sharing, no good-night kisses. And then, after the wedding, a kind of explosion of sensuality, mother and stepfather having no need to curb their ardour. Because it would be okay, wouldn't it, they were *married*, it was respectable, nothing to object to. A shock to the girl, wouldn't you say?"

"According to Hilary, it was pretty much like that." Burden began assembling in his mind the facts and details as Hilary Stacey had told them. "Sophie seems to have given him hell. Screamed at him, insulted him, then refused to speak to him at all. That went on for a week, and one evening she just didn't come home from school. Hilary Stacey didn't have time to get worried. Sophie phoned her and said she was with Mrs. Waterton and there she intended to stay."

"Why Mrs. Waterton?" Wexford asked.

"That's rather interesting in itself. Sophie is a very bright child, good at her school-work, always in the top three. And she does a lot of community service, visiting the elderly and the bereaved, that sort of thing. She does their shopping and sits with them. There's a blind woman she calls on and reads the newspaper to her. As well as this she does baby-sitting—she baby-sits for us—and she used to do a paper round, only her mother stopped that, quite rightly in my view; it's dangerous even in a place like this.

"Ann Waterton's in her sixties. She lost her husband in the spring and apparently it hit her very hard. There were no children. Sophie used to go to her house after school, just to talk, really. They seem to have got on very well."

"A girl of that age," Wexford said, "will often get on a great deal better with an older woman than with her own mother. I take it this Ann Waterton's no slouch—I mean, she's got something to give a lively intelligent fourteen-year-old?"

"According to Hilary, she's a retired teacher. In his last years she and her husband were both studying for Open University degrees, but she gave that up when he died. At one time she used to write the nature column for the Kingsmarkham *Courier*."

Wexford looked dubious. The car had joined the queue of vehicles lining up for the toll at the Dartford Tunnel. They were in for a long wait. Burden looked at his watch, a fairly useless exercise.

"One evening, about a month after George Waterton died, Sophie called round there. It was about nine but light still. She was on her bicycle. Hilary Stacey and Ann Waterton live about a mile apart, Hilary in Glendale Road—you know, the next street to me—and Mrs. Waterton in Coulson Gardens. Sophie couldn't make Mrs. Waterton hear, but the back door was unlocked and she went in, thinking she would find her fallen asleep over a book or the television.

"She did find her, in an armchair in the living-room, and she appeared to be asleep. There was an empty pill bottle on the table beside her and a tumbler that seemed to have contained brandy. Sophie acted with great presence of mind. She phoned for an ambulance and she phoned her mother. Of course Hilary hadn't yet married Martin Stacey, though she was planning to marry him, the wedding being fixed for August.

"Hilary got there first. She and Sophie managed to get Ann Waterton onto her feet and were walking or dragging her up and down when the ambulance came. As we know, they were in time and Ann Waterton recovered."

Wexford said unexpectedly, "Was there a suicide note?"

"I don't know. Hilary didn't say. Apparently not. She and Sophie had been very anxious it shouldn't appear as a suicide attempt but as an accidental taking of an overdose."

"Bit indiscreet telling you then, wasn't it?" said Wexford derisively. "Why did she tell you?"

"I don't know, Reg. It was all part of the background, I suppose. She knew I wouldn't broadcast it around."

"You've told *me*. And Donaldson's not deaf."

"That's all right, sir," said Donaldson, no doubt indicating his willingness to be the soul of discretion.

"I imagine everybody knew about it," said Wexford. "Or guessed. And after that she and this Mrs. Waterton became fast friends, is that it? The house in Coulson Gardens was the natural place for the girl to decamp to." He pondered for a moment or two as the car moved sluggishly towards one of the toll booths. "The mother might be able to get a care order made or a supervision order," he said. "She could try to get her made a Ward of Court. It's hardly a case for Habeas Corpus."

"She doesn't want to do that, and who can blame her? She wants the girl back living with her. Sophie's out of control, it's true; that is, her mother can't control her to the extent of making her come home, but she hasn't done anything wrong, she's broken no law."

"The danger," said Wexford, "with getting a care order for someone who's out of control might be that it contained a requirement for the subject, that is, Sophie Grant, to reside with a named individual—and suppose that named individual was Ann Waterton?"

The car began to head for London up the motorway.

From the tall, rather forbidding curtain wall of stone blocks rose thirteen towers. The arc lamps flooded them with white light and showed up the cloudy smoky texture of the sky behind, purplish, very dark, starless. In the great hall, which had lost its roof some six centuries before, and which was open to this heavy rain-threatening sky, a performance of Elizabethan music was under way, was drawing to its close just in time, thought Burden, before the heavens opened. He was there, sitting in the second row, because Jenny was singing in the choir.

This was the first time he had been to Myland Castle, a type of fortification (according to the programme) innovative in Europe in the twelfth century. It was a huge fortress containing the remains of gateways and garderobes and kitchens and tunnel-vaulted rooms and features called rere-arches. Burden was more interested in the castle than the concert. It was too late in the year, in his opinion, for outdoor performances of anything. The evening was damp and raw rather than really cold, but it was cold enough. The audience huddled inside sheepskin and anoraks.

It was a mystery why the organizers had picked on this place. Size alone must account for it, for the acoustics were so bad that the harpsichord was nearly inaudible and the sweet melodious voices seemed carried up into the sky where no doubt they could be clearly heard some two hundred feet in the air. As a soloist began on the final song, "Though Amaryllis Dance in Green," Burden let his eyes rove along the top of the walls and the catwalk between the towers. From the other side of the curtain wall, where the great buttresses fell steeply away to green slopes and a dry moat, the view across country must be very fine. Perhaps he would come back in the spring and bring Mark.

The applause was enthusiastic. Relief, they're glad it's all over, thought Burden, the Philistine. Jenny, coming up to him, laying an icy hand on his, said, "You couldn't hear, could you?"

Burden grinned. "We couldn't hear as much as we were meant to." He was astonished and pleased to see it was not yet nine. Time had passed slowly. He took his wife's arm and they ran for it to the car as the rain began.

The extreme youth of their baby-sitter had worried him the first time she came. That Sophie Grant would phone her mother in the next street, if there was any cause for alarm, did a lot to calm his fears. By the time she had sat for them three times he trusted her as entirely as he would have trusted someone three times her age. She might be fourteen but she looked seventeen. It was absurd, he reflected as he walked into his living-room, to think of her in the context of care orders, of being in need of supervision or protection.

She was sitting on the sofa, with her books beside her, writing an essay on unlined paper attached to a clipboard. Her handwriting was strong, clearly legible, slightly forwards-sloping. She looked up and said, "I haven't heard a sound from him. I went up three times and he was fast asleep." She smiled. "With his rabbit. He's inseparable from that rabbit."

"D'you want a drink, Sophie?" Jenny remembered she was a child. It was easy to forget. "I mean, hot chocolate or a cup of tea or something?"

"No, thanks, I'd better get off."

"What do we owe you?"

"Nine pounds, please, Jenny, three hours at three pounds an hour. I started at six-thirty, I think." Sophie spoke in a crisp and business-like way, without a hint of diffidence. She took the note and gave Jenny a pound coin.

Burden fetched her coat. It was a navy-blue duffle and in it she immediately shed a few years. She was a schoolgirl again, tall, rather gawky, olive-skinned and dark-haired, the hair long and straight, pushed behind her ears. The shape of her face and the blue eyes were her mother's, but she was prettier. She packed books and clipboard into a rather battered brief-case.

"I'll walk you home," said Burden. It was only round the corner, but these days you never knew. He had forgotten for the moment where home was for her now. She said,

"Coulson Gardens. It's a long walk."

Should he dispute it? Argue? "I'll drive you."

They were uncomfortable together in the car. Or Burden was uncomfortable. The girl seemed tranquil enough. It was cowardice, he thought, that kept him from speaking. Was he afraid of a fourteen-year-old?

"How long are you going to keep this up, Sophie?" he said.

"Keep what up?" She wasn't going to help him.

"This business of living with Mrs. Waterton, of refusing to go home to your mother."

For a moment he thought she was going to tell him to mind his own business. She didn't. "I haven't refused to go home," she said. "I've said I'll go home when he's not there. When she gets rid of him, I'll go home."

"Come on, he's her husband."

"And I'm her daughter. You're going past it, Mike, it's the house with the red gate. She loves him, she doesn't love me. Why should I go to live with someone who doesn't care for me?"

She jumped out of the car before he could open the door for her. A small slim woman with short grey hair was looking out of a front window, the curtain caught on her shoulder. She smiled, gave a little wave, a flutter of fingers. Burden thought, I can't just leave it, I can't miss this opportunity.

"What's Martin Stacey done, Sophie? Why don't you like him? He's a nice enough chap, he's all right."

"He made her deceive me. They pretended things. They both pretended he was going to look after us and earn money for us and *like* us both, not just her, not just want to be with her. And she pretended I was the most important person in the world to her. It was all false, all lies. I was nothing. He made me nothing and she *liked* it." She spoke in a low, intense voice that was almost a growl. A pause in which she drew a long breath, then, "Thanks for the lift, Mike. Good night."

She ran up the path and the door opened for her, but the figure of Mrs. Waterton was not visible.

On the way home he thought, it's as much that woman's doing as the girl's. Why does she give her a room? Why does she feed her? She ought to go away for a bit, shut up the house. She would if she had any sense of responsibility. He said something of this to his wife.

"Oh, think, Mike, how Ann Waterton must love it. She was all alone, a widow, no children, probably not many friends. People don't want to know widows, or so they say. And then suddenly along comes a ready-made granddaughter, someone who actually *prefers* her over her own mother and her own home. I'm not saying she deliberately encouraged Sophie, but I bet you she doesn't make any positive moves to send her home. It must have brought her a new lease of life. Did she look happy?"

"I suppose she did," said Burden.

"Well, then. And less than six months ago she was suicidal."

It was a fortnight before he saw Sophie's mother again. Once more she was spending the evening with Jenny, Martin Stacey being away on a protracted business trip abroad.

"He's glad to get away from me, I expect. It's been nothing but trouble ever since we got married. Of course he's been angelic, but how long can that go on? I'm always miserable, I cry every day, I'm always in a state, he can't put up with that forever. So I've decided what to do. You tell him, Jenny. Tell him what I'm doing."

Jenny said drily, "It's a case of if you can't beat 'em, join 'em. Hilary's idea is that the best thing for her to do is make friends with Ann Waterton."

"I've stopped arguing about it, I've stopped telling her she has to send Sophie home, and I've stopped threatening her."

"Threatening her?" said Burden, on the alert.

"I only mean telling her I'd get an injunction to stop her seeing Sophie. I don't suppose I ever would have. But now I've decided to *like* her. The way I see it, I don't have a choice. And if it works—well, oh, it's all in the air as yet, but I thought maybe we could all live together. If Sophie's that crazy about old Ann, the answer might be for us all to be together. Sell our houses and buy a big house for the lot of us."

Burden thought, but surely it's not that Sophie is specially "crazy" about Mrs. Waterton as that she is specially un-crazy about her stepfather. He did not care to say this aloud. It occurred to him that Hilary Stacey, if not exactly unhinged by all this, was becoming rather strange.

"So what's happening?" said Jenny. "You're inviting her to tea, are you? Taking her out for drives?"

"She can drive herself," Hilary said shortly. "This is deadly serious, Jenny, this is my life, my whole future existence we're talking about. You could say I've lost my only child."

Jenny poured her another glass of wine.

"I reason," said Hilary, "that if my daughter likes someone that much, I could like her too. After all, we used to be very close, Sophie and I, we used to like the same things, the same people, we had the same taste in clothes, we liked the same food. There's got to be something about old Ann that I can like. And there is, there is. I can see there's a lot more to her than I thought at first. I thought Sophie was flattered—you know, a sort of granny-substitute buttering her up and telling her how pretty and clever and mature she was, all that, but Ann's a very bright woman, she's very well-read. It's just a matter of my meeting her more than half-way."

"I wonder what that poor devil of a husband's going to say," was Wexford's comment when Burden retailed all this to him, "having a supererogatory mother-in-law shacking up with him."

"Hardly 'shacking up,'" Burden protested, "and it hasn't come to that yet. Personally, I don't think it ever will."

"Does her mother make her an allowance? Give her pocket money?"

"I don't know. I never asked."

"I was thinking of a scene from *The Last Chronicle of Barset*," said Wexford, who was rereading his Trollope. "The Archdeacon wants to know how to deal with a recalcitrant son. His daughter asks him if he allows her brother an income, and when he replies, yes, says,

'I should tell him that must depend upon his con-
duct.'"

"Does it work?" said Burden, interested in spite of
himself.

"No," said Wexford rather sadly. "No, it doesn't. I
shouldn't expect it to, not with anyone of spirit, would
you?"

An inquiry about an attack on a cyclist took
Wexford and Sergeant Martin to Myland Castle. It was
the fourth in a series of such assaults, each apparently
motiveless, for the amount of money the cyclists carried was negligible. Three were men, one a woman.
Two of the attacks happened by day, two after dark.
The only pattern discernible seemed to be that the
attacks increased in severity, the first, on the woman,
consisting in not much more than pushing her off her
bicycle and damaging the machine to make it tempo-
rarily unusable, but the fourth had put the victim into
intensive care with broken bones and a ruptured
spleen.

All these seemingly pointless acts of violence had
taken place in the Myfleet-Myland neighbourhood,
this last on the cycle path that led from the Myfleet
Road to Myland Village and passed on the outer side
of the castle moat. Wexford had already questioned
the staff at the castle. The purpose of this return visit
was to re-examine one of the guides. Two members of
the staff, those manning the south gate and the turnstile, claimed to have seen the victim, a frequent cyclist
on the path, but only the guide admitted to the
possibility of having seen the perpetrator. Just before
the castle closed to the public at four, he had been

standing in the gathering dusk on the curtain wall between the two south towers.

It was a fine day, a sunny island of a day in a week of fog and rain, and the number of visitors to Myland Castle was nearer a mid-summer than a December average. While Martin talked to the woman at the turnstile, Wexford went across the great hall in search of the guide. The two-o'clock tour had five more minutes to run. Wexford could see the group of about ten people standing on the battlements, the guide pointing across the meadows towards the Myland church, where the tombs of the castle builders were.

While he waited Wexford made his way to the remains of a chapel and hall embedded in the inner court. This had been a town rather than a dwelling-house, with gatehouses and barracks, almshouses and courts. From the passage along which he was walking, a flight of stone stairs led up onto the curtain wall and these he took, emerging into the fresh air but also to deep shadow. It was possible to walk round the battlements on this walkway, occasionally passing up and down steps inside the turrets. The wall on the inner side was high enough, it came up to his waist, but it was rather lower on the outer side, and crenellated. However, the path was wide, the wall was more than small-child height, and even a venturesome older person would have had to lean over and lose balance in order to fall.

Falling would be an atrocious thing, Wexford thought. The battlements here were like cliffs but with no merciful sea at their base. Their height was increased by the moat, a fifteen-feet-deep ditch, whose northern side at this point continued downwards the sheer slope of the castle wall. He walked along slowly, keeping in sight the guide, Peter Ratcliffe, and his group, now standing under the great bulwark of the gatehouse-flanking tower.

He was not alone on the walkway. He could hear a party with children mounting the staircase behind him, and in front, some twenty or thirty feet ahead, saw two women appear from the steps inside the first of the south turrets. It was probably his fancy that when she saw him—and saw also those behind him—the younger of the women whispered something to her companion and they turned back the way they had come. Most likely they had meant to turn back anyway and retrace their steps along the sunny side. An area of deep cold shade lay between them and Wexford.

He walked along and through it more quickly. Beyond the turret the sun began, and it was warm and benign on his face. The two women were still ahead of him and as he observed them, talking together, sometimes pointing across the fields or studying the guidebook the older one carried, he knew who they were. That was putting it rather too strongly perhaps. He guessed who they might be, he *thought* he knew. The bright fair hair of one of them told him, and her rather protuberant blue eyes, extraordinarily blue and clear, just as Burden had described them. As if she sensed his watchfulness, she turned round and those eyes cast their blue beam on him.

The other woman was small and slight, very upright, perhaps sixty-five, with short grey hair. Hilary Stacey and Ann Waterton. He was so sure that he wouldn't have hesitated to address them by their names. Inside the gatehouse tower the main exit staircase went down. He saw them enter the arch to the tower and by the time he had reached it they had begun the descent. Ratcliffe's party immediately appeared, heading in their turn for the exit staircase. Wexford pressed himself against the wall to allow their passage, and when the last of them was through, Ratcliffe came sauntering up, all smiles and helpfulness.

"Brain-picking time?" he said. "They tell me I'm needed to help you with your enquiries."

It was uttered in a facetious way, quotation marks very evident round the last words. Wexford said quietly, "Perhaps we can go a few yards along the walkway, Mr. Ratcliffe, to the place from which you saw the attacker."

A neighbour called the police. It was nine o'clock on a Friday. He had gone out into his front garden and heard a car engine running. The only car nearby was shut up in Ann Waterton's garage. He opened the garage doors and the first thing he saw was the length of hose attached to the exhaust, passing in through the driver's window.

He switched off the engine and pulled Ann Waterton out. Giving the kiss of life, what he, an elderly man, called "artificial respiration," had no effect. She was dead. When the police came they found the house unlocked but empty. On the table in the dining-room, in a sealed envelope marked "To the Coroner," was what they concluded was a suicide note.

"Where was the girl?" Wexford asked when Martin told him about it next day.

"Gone on a school trip to London," said Burden. "A theatre visit apparently. Shakespeare, something they were studying. They went in a coach, which didn't get back to Kingsmarkham until eleven-thirty."

"And Sophie, finding what had happened, at last went home to Mother?"

"It would seem so."

At the inquest a verdict was returned on Ann Waterton of suicide while the balance of her mind was disturbed. The suicide note, written in the firm, round, characterless hand of the primary-school teacher, was read aloud. *I cannot go on. Life has become a meaningless farce. I am totally alone now, with no prospect of things ever changing. I am unwanted, an unnecessary woman, a useless drag on society. It is better for everyone this way, and much better for myself. Ann Waterton.*

"Totally alone?" Burden said to Jenny. "She had Sophie, didn't she?"

"Sophie was going home."

"What? You mean, before all this happened, Sophie meant to leave her? To go home? She'd given in at last?"

"Hilary said so in evidence at the inquest. The coroner asked her about her daughter living with Ann and she told him how Sophie was returning home. She told me privately, between ourselves, that she and Sophie had had some talks. They had a talk with Ann there and some talks on their own and the upshot was that Sophie said, all right, she'd come home by Christmas and she made a few conditions, but the crux of it was she'd come home."

"Conditions?" Burden took his little boy on his knee. He was wondering, not for the first time, how he would feel in ten years' time if this child, this apple of his eye, upped and packed his bags and went to live in someone else's house. "What conditions?"

"Oh, they were to turn the attics into a sort of flat

for her. It's quite a big house. She was to have her own kitchen and bathroom, live separately. Hilary must have agreed. She'd have agreed to almost anything to get Sophie back."

"And Ann Waterton knew this?" Mark was thrusting a book under his father's nose, demanding to be read to. "Yes, just a minute; I will, I promise I will." He said to his wife, "She knew it and that's what she meant by being 'totally alone,' and being 'an unnecessary woman'?"

"I suppose so. It's rather awful, but it's nobody's fault. You have to think of it that if the girl hadn't gone there in the first place, Ann Waterton would be dead anyway. She'd just have died six months sooner. She was determined to kill herself."

Burden nodded. Mark had opened the book and was pointing rather sternly at the first word of the first line. His father began reading the latest adventure of Postman Pat.

"Anthony Trollope," said Wexford, "wrote about fifty books. It's a lot, isn't it? One of them, a not very well-known one, is called *Cousin Henry*. I've just finished reading it." He took note of the expression on Burden's face. "I know this bores you. I wouldn't be telling you about it if I didn't think it was important."

"Important?"

"Well, perhaps not important. Interesting. Significant. It gave me something to think about. Trollope wasn't what one would normally think of as a psychologist."

"Too long ago for that, wasn't it?" Burden said vaguely. "I mean, surely psychology wasn't invented till this century."

"I wouldn't say that. Psychology is one of those things that was always with us, before anyone gave it a name, that is. Like, well, linguistics, for instance. And 'invented' isn't quite the word. Discovered."

It was the end of the day. They were at a table in the saloon bar of the Olive and Dove. Earlier, Wexford had made an arrest, that of Peter Ratcliffe, the Myland Castle guide. His attacks on the cyclists he was unable adequately to account for, though he had fully confessed to all of them. The explanation he gave Wexford was a strange one, it almost pointed to a disturbance of the man's mind. His daily presence in the castle, year after year, day after day, had brought him to a curious identification with its former defenders. It impelled him to attack those he saw as intruders. Perhaps it would only have been a matter of time before the paying visitors appeared to him in the same light and he injured one of them.

Wexford didn't know whether he believed this or not. No court would. Burden had stared in incredulous disgust when Wexford repeated Ratcliffe's words. That was why—partly why—he had changed the subject onto *Cousin Henry*.

"Bear with me," he said, "while I give you a brief outline of the plot." Burden didn't exactly demur, not quite. His face was a sigh incarnate. Wexford said, "I promise you it's relevant." He added, "It even gets exciting."

Burden nodded. He looked reflectively into his beer.

"The old squire dies," Wexford began, "and leaves all his property to his nephew Henry. Or that's how it appears, that's what everyone thinks, and Henry comes into his inheritance. Then he finds a later will which leaves everything to his cousin Isabel. Henry's best bet is to destroy this will, but he doesn't. He daren't. He hides it in a place where he thinks it will be never be found, in fact in a book in the library, a book that is so boring no one would ever want to take it down and open it. Why doesn't he destroy it? He's afraid. It's an official document, an almost sacred thing, it exercises an awesome power over him, it's almost as if he's afraid of some unnamed retribution. Yet if he destroys it—a simple thing to do, though Henry, in his mind, discovers terrible difficulties in the way of doing this—if he does, all will be secure forever and he the undisputed man in possession. But he can't destroy it, he daren't. Good psychology, don't you think? People behave like that, inexplicably, absurdly, but that's how they behave."

"I suppose so. Thousands would. Have destroyed it, I mean. Most would."

"Not the law-abiding. Not the conventional. Someone like you wouldn't."

"I wouldn't have nicked it in the first place. What's the point of all this? You said there was a point."

"Oh, yes. The Stacey-Grant-Waterton affair, that's the point."

Burden looked up at him, surprised. "No wills involved in that, so far as I know."

"No wills," said Wexford, "but another sort of document, a sacred sort of document. A suicide note."

Wexford was silent for a moment, enjoying the look on Burden's face that was a mixture of incredulity and sheer alarm. "Let me give you a scenario," he said. "Let me give you an alternative to what actually happened, a lonely unhappy woman at last succeeding at taking her own life."

"Why have an alternative to the facts?"

"Just listen to a theory then. Ann Waterton didn't commit suicide. She had no reason to commit suicide. She was happy, she was happier than she had been since her husband died. She had found an affectionate, charming granddaughter, who *wanted* more than anything in the world to live with her."

"Wait a minute," said Burden. "Sophie may have been living with her, but she wasn't going to go on doing that. She was going home. She was going back to her mother and her stepfather."

"Was she? Do we have anyone's word for that but Hilary Stacey's?"

"She told the coroner under oath."

"Hmm," said Wexford. "D'you want another drink?"

"I don't think I do. I want to hear the rest of what you've got to say."

"All right. The fact is that we have no evidence that Sophie intended to go home but Hilary Stacey's word."

"Sophie herself. Sophie could presumably confirm it?"

Wexford smiled rather enigmatically. "Hilary Stacey's her mother. She may have been at odds with her, but I don't think she'd shop her own mother."

"Shop her?"

"Suppose Hilary Stacey murdered Ann Waterton . . . I saw them at Myland Castle about ten days ago. I recognized them from your description. If I hadn't been there, if so many visitors hadn't been there—an exceptional number for December, but it was an exceptionally nice day—I think Hilary—oh, yes, it's hindsight—was going to push Ann off that wall. It would have been, would have looked, like an accident. It was made impossible by the circumstances.

"Three days afterwards Sophie went on a school trip to a London theatre. Hilary was often at the house in Coulson Gardens; it would have been nothing out of the way for her to drop in during the evening. The next step was to give Ann a heavy dose of sleeping-pills. She would have made them both a drink, given her the pills in that. Ann was a small, slight woman, it looked to me as if she weighed no more than seven stone. Hilary Stacey, on the other hand, is tall and strong and no more than—what? Thirty-seven? Thirty-eight? She carried Ann out to the garage, by way of the communicating door from the house, sat her in the driving-seat, and fixed up that business with the hose-pipe and the exhaust.

"No doubt she supposed Sophie would find the body. An unpleasant thought. No mother would do that to her child? Perhaps not. Perhaps Hilary intended to come back later and find the body herself. In any event, the next-door neighbour found Ann Waterton."

Burden said, "It doesn't work, Reg. You're forgetting the suicide note. Ann left a note for the coroner."

"I'm not forgetting it. The suicide note is at the heart of all this. We have to go back to last May or June, whenever it was. Ann Waterton attempted to kill herself, but the attempt was frustrated by Sophie Grant and her mother. There was no suicide note—or was there? Has anyone heard of the existence of a suicide note? On the other hand, has the existence of such a note been denied? Let us postulate that there was such a note. On the mantelpiece or in a pocket of Ann's dress or by her bed. Remember that suicides, especially 'home' suicides, almost always leave a note."

"Yes, but we've discussed this. That first time Hilary and Sophie wanted to keep it dark that there'd been a suicide attempt. For Ann's sake."

"What are you saying, Inspector Burden? And you a policeman! Are you saying they *destroyed a suicide note* for no more reason than to protect the reputation of a woman who was then no more than an acquaintance? No, of course you aren't, and of course they didn't. It's quite possible indeed that Sophie knew nothing about it but that Hilary, spotting what it was, picked it up and took it away with her."

"But didn't destroy it?"

"No, no. Remember Cousin Henry. She took it. She had no prevision of any future need for it; Ann at that time had done her no harm and there was no hint that she would. She took it, as I say, and read it, as Cousin Henry read his uncle's will, and decided to tell no one about it. Ann had been found in time, Ann would survive. And, by the way, I'd suggest at that time the note was in its envelope but *unsealed*. Hilary later did the sealing.

"She preserved it. Not for any nefarious purpose then but simply because it had become an official document, a document of great weight and significance, fraught almost with magic. Perhaps she thought she would give it back to Ann one day. Ann would be happy again and they would—dare she expect it?— laugh about it together. But I think the real reason for preserving it was Cousin Henry's; she was *afraid* to destroy it. And why do so anyway? Easier than destroying it was to slip it inside a book in the way Cousin

Henry concealed the will, a book no one in the household was ever likely to want to read or even take down and look at.

"In Cousin Henry's case it was Jeremy Taylor's sermons. What book Hilary Stacey used we shall never know and it doesn't matter. Perhaps, anyway, she kept it in a drawer with her underclothes.

"But possession of the suicide note gave her the idea for Ann Waterton's murder. After she had put Ann into the car she had only to place the note on the table and, making sure she had left no fingerprints, return home and leave the body to be discovered."

Burden, who had listened to the last part of this in silence and with his head bowed, now looked up. He shook his head a little, but rather as if in wonder at human depravity than in any particular doubt at what Wexford had told him. It might be true, Hilary Stacey had been angry enough, desperate enough. He realized he had never really liked her.

"You'll never prove it," he said, and as he spoke he was confident Wexford would agree with him. Wexford would give him a rueful smile, accept the inevitable. His chief often, still, surprised him.

"I shall have a damn good try," said Wexford.

Staying out drinking wasn't Burden's way. It never had been. He was an uxorious man, a home-loving man. Anyway, he liked to be with his little boy before Mark went to bed; liked, if possible, to put him to bed himself. If the licensing hours hadn't changed from a cast-iron regularity to depend upon the whim of the landlord, he wouldn't have been able to have a beer with Wexford at ten to five. As it was, he was still early, though the evening was as dark as midnight. He walked home thinking about Hilary Stacey. It seemed to him unfortunate she had been Jenny's friend. How much, he wondered, did Jenny care for her? And should he tell Jenny something of all this?

It might be best to wait awhile, see what unfolded, see how Wexford progressed. There would be a point at which he would know the time had come to divulge horrors, undreamt-of intrigue. He found Jenny in an armchair by the fire, the child on her knee. Mark was in pyjamas and a blue dressing-gown of classic cut, piped in navy and tied with a silk cord. Jenny was reading to him, Beatrix Potter this time, the one about the kitten who traps a mouse in her pocket handkerchief, but the mouse escapes through a hole. Mark was mad about literature, he would soon be able to read himself. Rather gloomily, Burden saw a future with a son always talking about books.

Mark got down from Jenny's lap and came over to his father. Another adventure of some thwarted predator or enterprising rodent was demanded. While Burden was looking through the collection on the bookshelf, the doorbell rang.

After dark he answered the door himself to unexpected visitors. You never could tell. He went out into the hall, Jenny behind him with the boy, holding his hand because he was nearly too heavy to carry. Burden opened the door and the girl came in. She stepped in quickly and stood for a moment in the hall, a suitcase in each hand.

"I've come," Sophie said, smiling. "I'll cook for you, I'll look after Mark, I won't be any trouble. Don't bother to come with me, Mike, I'll just take these straight up to the spare room."